MW00810133

Beware the Orchids

A Shady Acres Mystery, Book 1

By Cynthia Hickey

Written by: Cynthia Hickey
Published by: Winged Publications

This book is a work of fiction. Names, characters, places, and incidents are the product of the author's imagination and are used fictitiously. Any resemblance to actual events, locales, or persons, living or dead, is coincidental.

ISBN-10:1-944203-06-0
ISBN-13:978-1-944203-06-1

Prologue

I still wore my wedding dress when I posted my resignation at Cooper Elementary. Not a strange thing considering I waited in the back room of a church for a groom to show up. One I doubted very much was actually going to attend the ceremony. Since he seemed so reluctant to marry me, I no longer wanted to teach in the same school in which he was principal. I typed my name, Shelby Hart, and hit send.

Things had gone south between us months ago. His leaving me at the altar shouldn't come as a big surprise. Still, I swiped the back of my hand against my tears and waited like a fool. If he showed, I'd take back my resignation.

My cell phone dinged, signaling a text message. Yep, it was from Donald telling me he'd changed his mind, we were making a big mistake, and he wished me the best. The jerk! I tossed my cell phone across the room, smiling with satisfaction as it fell in pieces.

"Mercy!" My mother, Sue Ellen, ducked as she entered the room. "What in Sam's Hill are you doing?"

I got to my feet. "I'm about to celebrate my freedom." I ripped off my veil and tossed it to her. "Send in my maid-of-honor. I need out of this dress. Donald backed out of the wedding."

"Good. I never did like him." Mom left.

Moments later, my best friend and maid-of-honor, Cheryl Leroix, rushed into the room and wrapped her perfume-lotioned arms around me, burying my face in her ample bosom. I was tiny, but my best friend was of Amazon proportions. Not fat, just…large. "I'm so sorry, but surely this doesn't come as a surprise?"

"Did everyone know he was going to jilt me, but me?" I returned her hug, then got to my feet. "Help me out of this dress and then take it to the consignment shop." My new life would begin. Where and doing what I had no idea.

1

*D*ressed in a black and white dress, adorned with a red sash and matching gardening boots, I marched through the front doors of Shady Acres retirement community to begin my new job as gardener slash event coordinator. The boots were to help me look the part. One phone call stating that I had been a third grade teacher and they'd hired me sight unseen. The director had laughed and said if I could handle thirty rowdy children I should be able to handle a retirement home of adults.

"You must be Shelby." A woman around the age of thirty met me at the door. "I'm Alice Johnson, esteemed manager and all around crazy woman. You have got to be the prettiest gardener I've ever seen."

"Thank you." I think. Her gaze flickered to my thin legs then back to the mound of black curls that wouldn't stay tied in a ponytail to save my life.

"You aren't bigger than a minute." She narrowed her eyes. "Are you sure you're up to the task?"

"Gardening has been my hobby for years, and you don't need to be big to plan events and plant flowers."

"True enough. Let me show you to your cottage and around the grounds. Then, you'll know where to park and unpack." Alice, dressed in a spotless suit of grey with a pink scarf tied around her neck, led me through a marble-floored foyer and through another set of double glass doors into a garden in desperate need of pruning and trimming.

A plump bottom and two legs stuck out from underneath a juniper bush.

"Maybelle Smith!" Alice propped her fists on her hips. "Crawl on out of there."

"Can't. I lost my teeth."

I bit my lip to keep from grinning. "Do these kinds of things happen often?"

"All the time." Alice tapped the older woman on the back. "Your teeth would not be under a bush."

A chubby woman with rosy cheeks and silver curls crawled from the bush and stood up, brushing off the knees of her knit pants. "I've checked everywhere except the outhouse."

"We don't have an outhouse, Maybelle. Perhaps you mean the greenhouse?"

"Yes. The place where flowers grow." She gave a toothless grin. "I'll go there now." She bustled off.

I couldn't help but let a giggle escape. "She's adorable."

"She's a menace. If she can't find her teeth, she'll steal someone else's. She's always where she doesn't belong." Alice continued down a flagstone path, her heels clicking in military precision. "You'll need a boatload of patience to work here, Shelby. I'd introduce you to some of our other characters, but I don't want you forming any opinions until you get to know them yourself. Here we are." She unlocked the door to a pretty little white cottage with a green tiled roof and pink climbing roses over the doorway.

I stepped inside my new two bedroom home. I could be very happy here. Wicker furniture filled the living room. A small glass table and four chairs took up the kitchen nook. In the master bedroom, a brass four-poster bed covered with a white Battenburg comforter invited one to lay back and relax. "It's beautiful."

"We did promise a furnished place, but if you want to substitute with anything of your own, just let us know and we'll have a volunteer switch it out for you, or Heath McLeroy, our handyman will help."

"Did I hear my name?"

I turned and lost all thought as a Chris Hemsworth lookalike strolled into my cottage. I closed my mouth so he didn't think I was a drowning fish. If this was the volunteer, I'd have to come up with a lot of reasons to use his services.

He grinned. "I'll be more than happy to help you with anything you need."

Oh, my, Father in heaven. Had I spoken my thoughts out loud? "Oh, well, I, uh…" I fished my keys from the little red purse hanging over my shoulder. "The red Volkswagon convertible is mine. Do you mind?"

"Not at all." He took the keys and ducked back out.

I sagged against the door. Be still my heart. I might have recently gotten out of a relationship, but my eyes deceived me into thinking I might be interested in the hunky handyman.

"Yes, he's very pretty. Most of the women here are ga-ga for him no matter how ancient they might be." Alice pointed at a stack of papers on the table. "Read over these, please. It gives your duties in great detail. If you have any questions, I'm number 2 on your phone. I'd best go help Maybelle find her teeth. See you at dinner, promptly at five."

I lowered myself into the nearest chair and flipped through the papers. Not too bad, once I got the garden in order. I had to plan a monthly grand event, a weekly social, and daily activities to get the residents out of their rooms and mingling. Alice wanted me to oversee the event she had planned for tomorrow. Bingo.

I wondered if the residents would like some of the games third graders played. Oh, well. A few moments on the internet and I'd have some ideas.

"I'm guessing you want help unloading the car?" Heath carried in a large suitcase. "And a small moving truck just pulled up. I directed them back here."

I jumped to my feet. "Yes, thank you." I had no idea where I would put all my things. It looked like most of it would go in my mother's garage after all. The clothes would have to somehow fit in the closet. Perhaps I could turn the second bedroom into a giant walk-in closet. "Just put everything in the guest room." I pulled five dollars out of my purse and held it out to him.

He laughed, the sound deep and rumbling. "I don't take tips." He shook his head and, still laughing, headed to the back bedroom.

Great, Shelby. Way to make an impression. I headed for the small kitchen, surprised to find the refrigerator fully stocked. There were no dishes in the cupboards, as I'd specified, so plenty of room for my cheery yellow and blue plates. A girl needed to be surrounded by pretty things, right? No plain white for me.

Soon, my little cottage was packed with two other muscular men and I was running out of space. Maybe I could use some of my things as prizes for Bingo. I had several stuffed animals I no longer needed, given to me by Donald. A bracelet, a necklace, the list was long of items he'd given me and I would do well to get rid of. Sweet. I had a plan.

"That little room is packed." Heath leaned against the table. "My cottage is a few doors down. If you need anything let me know. See you at dinner." He flashed another breath-stopping grin and followed the movers out the door.

The man was going to be a distraction. One I didn't want. After five years with Donald, I didn't want to think about another man. Heath would make that vow near to impossible to keep.

Having a good idea of my job duties, I decided to stroll the gardens and check out the greenhouse before heading to the dining room. At one time, someone had put a lot of work into the Shady Acres garden. The flagstone path alone was a labor of love, showcasing blues, greens, and gray stones. The evergreen bushes would be divine trimmed into exotic animals. I'd taken a class on that one summer and couldn't wait to give it a whirl. Overgrown rose bushes and other flowers simply needed pruning or replanting. I rubbed my hands together. I'd have my lovely striped boots dirty in no time. Good thing they're made of rubber. Any job goes easier if you look and feel good.

The greenhouse rose in the distance. The sun's rays sparkled off the glass like diamond dust. I pulled open the door and stepped into the musty interior.

Orchids! I rushed down the aisle, cradling a blossom between my fingers. This is the job I was born to do. While teaching had been fulfilling, I'd thought nothing of breaking my contract and paying back the remainder after Donald ditched me. I should have gotten into gardening a long time ago. Plants didn't reject a person. No, they filled the world with their beauty and scent.

I made note of where the tools I'd use were kept, where the water spigot was and turned to leave when I caught sight of Maybelle's feet sticking out from under one of the work benches. Her dirty fingers were curled around a small hand-held gardening shovel. "Lost your teeth again?"

No answer.

"It's me, the new gardener and event coordinator, Shelby. Do you need help?"

Maybelle didn't move.

My nerves tingled as I squatted next to her. Lying on its side was a box of rat poison. "Maybelle?" I grabbed her legs and pulled her out. Her lips were pulled back in a grimace over gums too swollen to hold the teeth lying loose in her mouth. I stumbled backward and screamed.

2

Still screaming, I got to my feet and darted from the greenhouse. Running toward me was Heath, with Alice teetering on her heels a few feet behind. Then, a curious look on her face was my…mother? And grandmother? Could the day get any stranger?

"What's wrong?" Heath gripped my shoulders and peered into my eyes. "Shelby? Stop screaming and tell me what happened? Did you see a snake?"

"What?" I frowned. "No, I'm not afraid of snakes. Maybelle is dead under the orchid plants."

His eyes widened right before he released me and dashed into the greenhouse. "Call 911!," he yelled.

Alice, breathing hard, punched in the numbers on her cell phone and told the operator about me finding the body. Alice glared at me as if I were the one who'd caused the upheaval in her day.

I returned her sharp look, regaining my senses, and turned to my mother. "What are the two of you doing here?"

"Your grandmother wanted to come." Mom hugged me. "She's decided it's time for a retirement apartment."

"What better place than right where my Shelby lives." My over-perfumed, red-haired grandmother, who fancied herself a Lucille Ball look-a-like, wrapped me and Mom in a hug. "This place might just be exciting enough for me. I'll take it. You say there's a dead body in there?" She motioned her head toward the greenhouse.

"It's horrible. I've never seen anything so…bad." I rested my head on her bony shoulder. From as far back as I could remember, breathing in the combination of Taboo cologne and cigarette smoke had meant Grandma was there to make everything better. "Are you really going to live here?"

"I think so. The cottages are adorable. I can help you plan the events. We'll have a ball." She stepped back, holding me with straight arms and stared into my eyes. "I think you need me."

Sirens wailed up the driveway, cutting short our conversation. Alice stepped forward to greet the two officers marching toward us.

"You reported finding a dead body?" The older one, a man resembling Ted Danson, glanced at Alice while continuing toward the greenhouse.

"She did." Alice pointed at me. "I haven't stepped foot inside there."

"You didn't make it there when you were looking for Maybelle earlier?" I remembered her saying she was heading there.

"I didn't make it that far, no." She looked at me as

if to ask what I was insinuating.

"Ma'am." Officer Dan…uh, Lawrence, according to his badge, took me by the arm and pulled me to the side. "The body?"

"Under the orchids." I pointed as Heath joined us.

"Poor Maybelle."

The officer sighed. "Please tell me you didn't touch anything."

"Not a thing." Heath shook his head.

"I dragged her from under the shelf," I volunteered.

"Don't say anything unless it's the result of a direct question." Grandma crossed her arms. "I thought I taught you that." Then, apparently thinking the officer handsome, she batted her fake eyelashes.

The younger officer, Officer Springer, headed into the greenhouse. By then, an ambulance had arrived and two paramedics carried one of those boards they carry bodies on, and followed the officer.

Officer Lawrence glanced at Grandma and smiled. "That isn't necessarily the wisest thing, Mrs…?"

"Grayson." Grandma cocked her head. "Ida Grayson."

I cleared my throat. "Don't you have some questions for me, Officer?"

"Yes." He transferred his attention to me. "What is your position at Shady Acres?"

"I'm the new gardener and event coordinator. I was checking out the grounds and greenhouse when I found…Maybelle. Why would her gums be swollen? Oh, and there's a box of rat poison next to her. Do you think she ingested some?" How horrible.

"We won't know anything until the autopsy, ma'am. Your name?"

"Shelby Hart. Ida is my grandmother."

"Today is Miss Hart's first day," Alice spoke up. "We do a thorough background check before hiring someone. She has no criminal record."

I noticed she didn't mention we didn't have a face-to-face interview. I'd sent the resume and referrals over the internet and did the interview over the phone. "I don't actually start work until tomorrow."

Alice glanced at her watch. "It's almost dinner time. The residents get cranky if dinner isn't served on time. Will you need me?" She glanced at Officer Lawrence.

"Not at the moment. I'll find you later."

She clip-clopped her way to the dining hall. "Don't be late, Shelby. I want to introduce you."

For one of her residents dying what looked like a painful death, she didn't seem to have a lot of empathy. I took a deep breath and turned my attention back to the officer. "I don't really have anything more to tell you." I averted my eyes from the black bag on the gurney containing Maybelle. "I met her a few hours ago while she was looking for her teeth under a bush. Then, I found her here. I guess she found her teeth. They were lying on her tongue." I shuddered.

"Sounds to me like she ate some poison." Grandma studied her peach colored nails. "The question here is whether she did so of her own accord."

"Why would you think that?" Officer Lawrence frowned. "You haven't seen the victim, have you? Why jump to this conclusion?"

"I watch a lot of crime shows on television. That's how my mind works. Did someone mention dinner. Are you staying Sue Ellen?"

Her question pulled my quiet mother from her stupor. “Oh, I don’t know if I can eat after all this.”

“Of course you can. There will be plenty of food. You can have that poor woman’s share.”

My gaze clashed with my mom’s startled one. “Not cool, Grandma.”

She waved a hand. “When I die, I don’t expect people to stop eating.”

Officer Lawrence rubbed his chin, high spots of color appearing on his cheeks. “Ladies, I need your contact information in case we have further questions, then you’re free to go.”

We gave our names, addresses and phone numbers. With a nod to me, and a smile at Grandma, Officer Lawrence joined his partner in the greenhouse.

Should I stay and supervise them? They were cops after all, and might resent me hanging around. I glanced at a pale-faced Heath. “Should we stay?”

“No, they can handle this.” He crooked his arms. Mom slipped her hand in one, Grandma in the other.

“You are a doll. I hope you work here,” Grandma said.

“I’m the handyman.”

“I’m sure you are.”

He glanced, red-faced at me. The poor man. His face changed colors faster than a chameleon.

“Let’s go eat,” Grandma said. “We have a mystery to solve. I’ve always fancied myself to be a red-haired Agatha Christie.”

Oh, no.

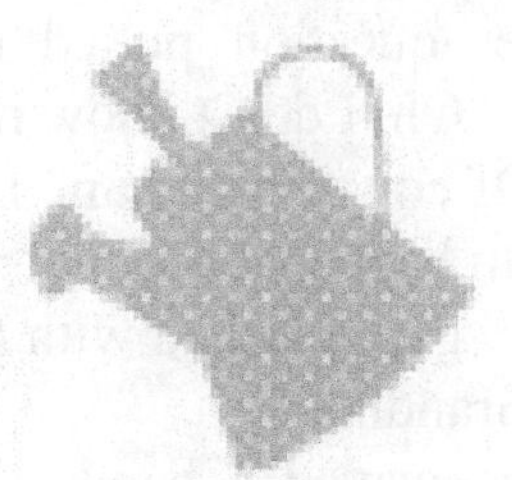

3

"You may sit as a guest at the employee table," Alice told Grandma when we entered. "Or anywhere among the residents. We'll get you checked in after supper. You have the last cottage available. Oh." The corners of her lips turned down. "I guess Maybelle's will be available soon." She clomped away.

"Some people do not know how to walk in heels without looking like a cow." Grandma plopped down at an empty table. "Sit, Sue Ellen, before you fall."

Mom shook her head. "I can't get over this day. First, you want to move and leave me, then Shelby finds a dead body. It's too much."

"You don't need me around anymore, and you cramp my style. The last time I brought a man home you gave him the third degree as if we were sixteen." Grandma glanced around the room. "Look at all the eligible men here. Why would I want to stay with you?"

I choked back a laugh and pretended to cough. The

men of Shady Acres had no idea the danger in their midst. I was tempted to stand up and yell, "Run for your lives."

"Living with you was like living with a teenager." Mom headed for the buffet.

Grandma followed. "I'm too old to need a chaperone."

"Those two are characters." Heath sat next to me.

My body flushed. "Especially Grandma."

"Aren't you hungry?" His blue eyes focused on me and increased the room's temperature by ten degrees.

"I'll wait for the piranhas to get their's first." I sighed. "Do people die unexpectedly around here often?"

"Not under suspicious circumstances." He shrugged. "Heart attacks, stroke, things like that."

"You think Maybelle's death is suspicious?"

He shrugged. "The way the cops were acting, it's a good deduction. At least they're treating the greenhouse like a crime scene. I don't think you'll be allowed access for a few days."

I gasped. I found the body. What if they considered me a suspect? I thought Donald jilting me at the altar was a bad thing. This was much worse. I folded my arms and rested my head on the table.

"Not a very good first day, was it?" Heath patted my back. "Come on. Let's hit the buffet. You'll feel better with something in your stomach."

I lifted my head and let him lead me to the long line. Today's theme was Mexican food. The buffet had everything one needed for tacos, nachos, and loaded burritos. I settled for two tacos, grabbing a diet coke on my way. As we finally reached the end, I grabbed a

Sopapilla. Then another. I stayed on the verge of being too skinny and was blessed with a high metabolism. It drove my best friend nuts.

"It looks like I'm getting dessert early," Grandma said as we approached the table. "Handsome, you sit next to me."

He grinned and gave me a wink. "It's Heath, ma'am."

"Of course it is. A man like you wouldn't have a sissy name like Hank." She lifted a glass of red wine. "The doctor said a glass of wine a night was good for my heart, so I drink two, just to be safe."

Heath laughed, the sound ringing across the dining room and attracting the attention of the residents. "You, Miss Ida, are good for my heart."

"Oh, you flirt." She blushed. Grandma actually blushed.

"Are you the one who found Maybelle?" A woman with pink tinted hair and wearing a bright yellow jumpsuit leaned over my shoulder. "I need to talk to you. Eight o'clock by the gazebo." She straightened and left.

"That's Birdie," Heath said. "She's a bit of a…character. Sees a conspiracy wherever she goes."

"Should I meet with her?" I picked up a taco.

"I'll go with you," Grandma offered. "You can't trust a woman with hair that color."

"I think your moving here is a bad idea," Mom said. "It isn't safe and there is too much trouble for you to find."

"Oh, hush, Sue Ellen. You need to learn how to live a little." Grandma downed what was left in her wine glass. "Where can I get another glass?"

"They only allow each resident one glass in the dining room." Heath cut into a carne asada. "If you want more, you'll have to buy it and put it in the fridge in your room."

"Good thing I have some in the van with my things. That's something a girl shouldn't run out of. You don't mind helping me unpack after supper, do you?"

"It will be my pleasure."

While my sixty-five-year-old Grandmother flirted with a man half her age, I surveyed the others in the room. What if Maybelle had been murdered? I didn't know enough about her to have a motive of any kind. Had her search for her teeth taken her somewhere she shouldn't have gone? Maybe she'd seen something she shouldn't have. Would people in a retirement community have something to hide that would warrant murder?

I shook my head. My over-active imagination was working overtime. A new job should take care of that. I didn't need to stick my nose where it didn't belong.

After supper, the four of us traipsed out to Grandma's van. She handed out orders like a drill sergeant then went to sign up for her cottage. While I was in number 7, she was in number 13. A number she swears is good luck. The best luck I had was that she wouldn't be living right next door to me.

By the time Mom had the van driven to Grandma's cottage, Grandma had re-joined us. "Wait until I go in first," Grandma said. "I have to get a feel for the place in order to know where to put things."

I peeked into the building after her. It looked almost identical to mine.

"Too much white." Grandma shook her head. "I need color. Good thing I have several doo dads to brighten the place up."

I knew that by morning, the cottage would resemble a rainbow inside. It wouldn't be Grandma's place if it didn't. There would be reds, blues, purples, and animal print everywhere.

"Where do you want all these boxes?" Heath squeezed past me, a large box balanced on his shoulder.

"In the kitchen nook. Bring the one that says fridge to me right away." Grandma took a deep breath. "I need my wine before we meet with Pink Hair."

"Her name is Birdie." I took a box from Mom and set it on the table, then headed to the van to help unload.

At five minutes to eight, I hugged Mom goodbye, thanked Heath for his help, and headed down a path illuminated with cheery lanterns to a gazebo strung with white lights. Birdie sat on a bench and leaped to her feet when we arrived.

"Thank you for coming. Maybelle was my friend."

"I'm sorry for your loss." I motioned for her to sit and took a seat next to her. "What did you want to meet about?"

She glanced around as if someone might be listening, then leaned close. "Now, she was my friend, but she was also a little..." she twirled her finger around her head. "Still, if she repeated something more than once it would behoove a person to listen. Now, just the other day, Maybelle told me someone here wasn't who they claimed to be."

"How would she know?"

"That woman got around, I tell you. Always

looking for her teeth, even when they were in her mouth. But sometimes…she left them places. Places people could get to them. I heard she was poisoned. What if someone put that poison on her dentures? Huh?"

"Who told you she was poisoned?" I glanced at Grandma, who shook her head.

"I might have spoken of it to your mother in the ladies room," Grandma said. "No one was in there. I promise. I always look under the stalls before I gossip."

Merciful God in heaven give me strength. "You can't be talking about a live police investigation. Do you want to get me arrested?"

"Oh, you're already the number one suspect. You found the body." Grandma grinned. "Remember, I'm full of knowledge from television."

Maybelle was no longer the craziest person in the community. Grandma was.

A twig snapped in the trees behind us.

"Duck!" Grandma dropped to the wood-slated floor.

Birdie followed.

I turned and listened. A squirrel scampered from the trees. "You're safe, unless it was a squirrel that killed Maybelle. It's been a long day. We should go to bed." I helped the other women to their feet.

"You found her." Birdie crossed her arms. "You're the event coordinator and gardener. You can go places I can't. I want you to find out who killed her."

"We don't know there was foul play."

"I know it in my gut."

"Fine. I'll see what I can find out. Do you want me to walk you home?" If I really was the prime suspect, as

Grandma thought, it wouldn't hurt to nose around a little.

"Would you? I don't want to be the killer's next victim."

I rolled my eyes. Things had gotten terribly out of hand.

"We're Cagney and Lacey, Ives and…whoever that other woman is. Sherlock and Doctor Watson." Grandma was way too eager to stick her nose into other people's business. "First thing tomorrow, we compare notes."

"We don't have any notes." I turned to follow Birdie down the path to her cottage. After making sure no boogieman hid under her bed, I rushed to get Grandma home so I could get to my own place and soak in a bubble bath.

"Good night, love." Grandma kissed me on the cheek. "See you at breakfast. We're going to have so much fun together. Maybe I'll ask your mother to move in with me. Do you think they'll allow it? Nah. I'm a free bird. I changed my mind. She can spend the night occasionally." She stepped inside and closed the door.

She exhausted me. Shoulders slumped, I trudged to my cottage. On the doorstep was a basket full of fruit and a note that said Welcome. I lifted it, unlocked my door, and set it on the dinette table. While the gift was thoughtful, all I wanted was a hot bath.

I shed my clothes and filled the tub with hot water and gardenia scented bubbles. Lowering myself into the water, I reached for the book I'd placed on the counter. A nice soak, a lovely romance novel, and I'd be ready for bed.

While I soaked, I thought over the last few weeks. I

wasn't as upset over Donald as I should be. I'd been doing what was expected after a long engagement, and greedy for the gifts he'd showered on me, to be honest. As an influential member of the community, he had to keep up appearances after all, and a trophy girlfriend made him look good. It was for the best that we weren't getting married, and I vowed not to dwell on it any longer.

My thoughts drifted to today. In the course of a few hours, I'd gotten a bipolar manager, a dead body, a hunky coworker, and Grandma. Life would not be boring in the least.

When the bath water cooled, I realized I hadn't read a single page in my book and climbed out of the tub. I dried off and donned a pair of cotton pajama pants and a tank top, then headed for the gift basket.

Oranges, apples, bananas and a pineapple. Yum. I reached for an apple, my hand pausing mid-air. I checked the note card. No name. If Maybelle had been murdered, how did I know this so-called gift wasn't from her killer? I couldn't take any chances. I hefted the basket and headed for the dumpster at the end of the walkway.

"You're out late." Alice glared at me, arms crossed.

"Just taking out the garbage."

"You're throwing away my gift?" Her eyes widened.

Uh-oh. "No, what? Where is my head? I didn't mean to bring this. You sent it? Thank you." I realized I was rambling and clamped my lips shut.

"I'm hoping we can be friends, Shelby, but you're an odd duck for sure." She shook her head and headed for the common building.

Since I seriously doubted Alice would kill one of her residents or employees, at least I hoped not, I bit into an apple and hoped for the best. Maybe I should have washed it first. Would hot water take care of poison on fruit?

4

Since I woke up the next morning, the apple must not have been laced with poison. I still had my teeth, the sun was shining, and I was officially on the job.

I dressed in a cute little dress that fluttered around my knees when I walked, a pair of matching rain boots, in case I trudged through the dirt. I had the cute little rubber boots in almost every color and style. A splurge I'd made when taking the new job. I locked my cottage in preparation of heading to the dining room for breakfast and waved at Grandma as she exited her cottage a few doors down.

"How did you sleep, love?" She gave me a kiss and linked her arm with mine. "That's a lovely dress, but the boots just don't work."

"I'm a gardener, Grandma. They work just fine."

"You have the strangest fashion sense, but I love you anyway."

I eyed her leopard print leggings and oversized black blouse. To each their own, I always said.

"The crime scene tape is still up on the

greenhouse," Grandma said. "I went by there, hoping to get a peek, but even I know stepping inside while the tape is there would be a crime."

I could only pray the flowers wouldn't die before I could tend to them. "Would you like to be the Bingo caller at tonight's game? I'm giving away some of the things Donald gave me as prizes."

"The necklace with the lion's head?"

"Yes." I'd always thought the large necklace hideous.

"Then, no. I prefer to win the necklace."

"If you want it that bad, you can have it. I've other things to give away." Actually, the necklace would fit her gaudy style very well.

"Okay. I'll be the caller. What fun! That'll put me front and center where everyone will wonder who the new gal in town is. I'm sure to catch a beau." She patted my hand and pulled away. "I won't be sitting with you this morning. I need to mingle." With that, she clomped away and pushed open both double doors, making a grand sweeping entrance. I'd always thought Grandma belonged in old-age Hollywood. She had the glamour.

"Good morning." Heath's deep voice washed over me.

I smiled. "Good morning."

"Ready for your first day?"

"I am, although there isn't a lot to do with the greenhouse out of commission. Still, I can do some trimming before tonight's activities."

"There will be plenty to keep you busy. Once all the residents find out you've been hired, you'll be swarmed with ideas from hopefuls. They'll all want their party idea to be the one chosen."

Maybe she could set up a suggestion box. That way, she wouldn't have to deal with all the people chasing her down. She could draw a few suggestions each month and keep it all non-personal.

Heath opened the door for her and let her enter first. The aroma of pancakes and bacon greeted her along with the sounds of silverware clanking, laughter, and the occasional belch.

"That would be Harold Ball. He prides himself on being the best belcher in Shady Acres." Heath pointed to a pudgy, bald man.

Every time the man belched, Grandma giggled. Good grief.

I followed Heath to the buffet, filling a plate with biscuits and gravy, then took a seat at the employee table with Heath, Alice, and a few people I didn't know.

"These are two of our house cleaning staff," Alice said, pointing to the two young women. "The blond is Amber and the brunette Becky. They've been tending the herb garden until we hired you."

An herb garden? Heath was right. I'd have more than enough work to keep me busy. "An herb garden, the grounds, activities, and the greenhouse. Is there anything else I need to add to my list?"

Alice tapped a manicured nail against her teeth. "Did you not read the papers I gave you?"

"Not all of them." The stack was two inches thick. It would take more than one night to get through it all. Especially when the prior evening was taken up with a death. "I'll make that a priority."

She nodded. "Everything set for Bingo?"

"Yes. I even have prizes."

"Wonderful! We've never had those before. I'll put the word out. We'll have a full house. The games and activities are all held in this room. We have a portable stage we use to put the caller up high."

"My grandmother has volunteered." I cut into a biscuit.

"That's fine, but don't play favorites. You'll need to include other residents on occasion."

Every time the woman spoke, I felt as if I were being scolded. I'd do my job well, and I'd do it my way. I'd signed a year contract. If she didn't like the way I did things, she could say so at the end of that time.

Birdie waved at me from across the room. I excused myself and rushed to her side.

She pulled me into the small hallway that led to the restrooms. "Did you find out anything?"

"I haven't had time."

She frowned. "Oh. I thought you might make solving the crime a priority."

"We don't know that there was a crime." I felt like a broken record. "And my priority is my job."

"I'm telling you there is a crime. Someone wanted Maybelle dead and put poison on her dentures." Birdie stomped her foot. "The longer you take, the more likely someone else will die."

"Shouldn't we let the police handle things? They're much more qualified than I am."

"But you have an in. You can mingle here and no one will suspect a thing." She narrowed her eyes. "I'm counting on you." She whirled and barged through the restroom door.

Resigned to yet another task on my to-do list, I told myself I'd see whether I could find out anything at Bingo.

~

"Speak clearly and concisely, Grandma." I handed her the laminated sheet of rules. "Read this out loud before we start the game." I turned and glanced at a packed room. A lot of people wanted to win the feather earrings, one hundred dollars, and a crystal vase I'd brought. Not to mention smaller dollar amount prizes.

"I'm perfectly capable of calling out numbers, Shelby. I graduated high school a long time ago, but I haven't forgotten." Grandma rolled her eyes and read the rules. "When you call Bingo, wave your arms and shout Bingo!"

One little old lady near the portable stage jumped in her seat and clasped a hand over her heart. I put a hand on her shoulder to calm her. "Perhaps you'd be better off further away?"

"No, dear. I want to be able to hear. I just wasn't expecting her to be so…loud."

I grinned and started to mingle. Not only to eavesdrop, but to make sure everyone's needs were met.

"O 72!" Grandma sang the number as if she were on a Broadway stage.

"Oh, she's a riot!" One of the residents daubed her paper with a flourish.

I chuckled and continued my rounds. Heath, obviously roped into service by Alice, manned a popcorn machine. I returned his smile and wave and leaned against a table after hearing one of the players mention Maybelle's name.

"She was a loon." One old man said. "Always getting into tight spots. One time, I caught her in my bathroom. She'd gotten confused as to which cottage was hers. Scared me to death to see her sleeping in my tub. In my tub!"

"That's why you lock your door, even in Shady Acres," another man said. "Looney Tunes all over the place."

A woman dressed to the nines in a lilac suit and pearls, leaned across the table. "I heard someone might have killed her."

"Nah." The first man daubed two of his papers. "She was harmless enough. Harmless!"

"She was nosy." Man number two said. "My guess…she put that big nose of hers in somebody's business and they offed her."

"No," Mrs. Pearls gasped. "I can't live here with a killer among us."

Someone at the next table shushed them. She had to be hard of hearing indeed if she needed them to stop whispering so she could hear Grandma's singing shouts of the numbers.

There was more gossip and speculation about what happened to Maybelle, but no concrete evidence I could take to the police. By the time we were on our third game, I was tired of roaming the large room and made my way to the popcorn machine.

Heath had me a bag ready before I stopped. "Saw you coming." He gave me a dimpled grin. "You look exhausted."

"I am." I tossed a few pieces of popcorn into my mouth. "White cheddar?"

"Your Grandma told me it was your favorite."

"Hmm. Bless her heart. I love it." I slipped off my shoes, perched on a nearby stool, and ignored the peeved glances sent my way by Alice. I hadn't noticed *her* traveling the room. Instead, she sat at a corner table and worked on papers. "There's a lot of discussion in the room about Maybelle. Whether she was murdered or not."

"If you're going to start asking questions, Shelby, be careful." Heath handed a man a bag of popcorn. "Even the elderly are capable of despicable acts of violence."

"You sound as if you'd had experience." I studied his face.

"Last year, two of the residents got into a fight and one stabbed the other five times. Wanted to make sure he was good and dead, he said." Heath shook his head. "We hate to think of such things in places like Shady Acres, but man will be man."

"Birdie has asked me to solve Maybelle's murder."

"Why?"

"She said I had access that she doesn't, and that the residents will talk to me easier than the police. Besides, Grandma thinks it will be fun."

"It'll be dangerous." He put a hand on my shoulder.

My skin heated from his touch. "I'm just asking a few questions. I'm most likely the prime suspect anyway."

"You're the primary person of interest." His eyes clouded with worry. "I heard the officers talking last night. They're curious as to why hours after the new gardener arrived, a woman was killed."

The popcorn sat like a rock in my stomach.

Perhaps I should up my investigation. Find something to give Officer Lawrence that would take the target off my back. Or would it put a bigger target for the killer? I sighed and pushed off the stool, slipping my feet back into my boots. I no longer cared who won the prizes I'd donated. I only wanted to return to my cottage and do something to take my mind off Maybelle.

By the time the games were over and the room cleaned and prepared for breakfast, it was almost ten o'clock. Grandma left right after, her arm linked with the belcher king, Harold. I didn't want to speculate what their plans were. Not with the way Grandma was leaning on him and giggling. I shuddered.

"I'll walk you to your cottage," Heath said. "If you're determined to investigate Maybelle's death, I don't want you out alone after dark."

"That's sweet, and I accept your offer, but Maybelle was killed in the middle of the afternoon. *If*, she was killed." I still didn't want to believe anything other than a horrible accident had occurred. A bit of minor investigating would prove I was right. I was certain of that fact.

Heath walked by my side on the way to my cottage. At the door, he took my key and unlocked the door for me. "Good night, Shelby." His eyes glimmered in one of the lamps lighting the path.

Forgive me, but I wanted him to kiss me. I wanted it badly. After Donald, I felt less a woman. A kiss by a man as handsome as Heath would help restore some of my self-esteem. Instead, he patted my shoulder and left me alone. Most likely a good thing since I was about ready to initiate the kiss myself and look like a fool.

5

My cell phone rang the next morning while I was in the shower. As soon as I'd finished, I wrapped in a towel and returned my best friend, Chery's call. "Hey, what's up?"

"Just calling to hear about the new job."

I sat on the sofa and propped my feet on the coffee table. "First day on the job I found a dead body in the greenhouse and met the world's sweetest and most handsome handyman. Second day on the job, Grandma sang numbers at a Bingo game while I mingled looking for clues as to who might have killed a toothless woman."

Cheryl was silent for a few moments. "Is the toothless woman the same victim or were their two murders?"

"Just one, thank God. The pink haired friend of the dead lady wants me to investigate because I can go everywhere around here. She's convinced her friend was murdered and did not accidentally drop her teeth into rat poison, then put them in her mouth." Which, if I thought about it, didn't seem at all plausible.

"Wow. Can I come live with you, because teaching isn't near as exciting?"

"Sure. Don't you have spring break next week?"

Cheryl laughed. "Seriously? Are we going to investigate a possible murder together? Heck. Today's the last day of school for break. I'll be there by four."

"See you then." Excitement swelled inside me. I'd glanced through the stack of papers on my desk last night and saw that we could have guests. Whether Maybelle died suspiciously or not, Cheryl and I would have a blast playing Nancy Drew and Bess.

A knock sounded at the door and I rushed to answer. With a sweep, I pulled the door open. "Good morning!"

Heath grinned, his gaze sweeping over me. "Good morning to you, too."

For Pete's sake. I was so excited about Cheryl coming to help me, I'd forgotten I was only wearing a towel. I tried my best to act cool, leaning against the door jamb. "What's up?" My foot slipped and down I went. The towel slipped. Merciful heavens! I grabbed what was left of my dignity, scrambled to my feet, and dashed for the bathroom.

I glanced in the mirror at my flaming cheeks and splashed cold water on my face. How would I ever face Heath? Maybe he'd be gone by the time I came out. No, I wasn't the lucky type.

I dressed in denim shorts, a yellow blouse tied at the waist and canary yellow rain boots with blue ducks on them. I was as ready as I'd ever be. I took a deep breath, chose to ignore what Heath may or may not have seen, plastered on a smile, and opened the bedroom door. "How can I help you?"

He bit his lip in a vain attempt at hiding his grin. "I overheard something last night after leaving your cottage and thought you might be interested."

"About Maybelle?"

He nodded. "After I left here last night, I heard Belcher, I mean Harold talking to your Grandmother about Maybelle. He said there were people here signing a petition to get her evicted because of her always being where she wasn't supposed to be."

"Now, she's dead." I dropped onto the sofa. "I get closer and closer to believing her death wasn't an accident." I locked gazes with him. "What could she have seen or heard to cause someone to kill her?" I needed to get my hands on a list of all the residents and start googling some names.

"What are you doing?" Heath's brows lowered. "Were you serious about investigating?"

"Yes. My best friend is coming to stay for a few days, and she'll help me. We use to play Nancy Drew all the time when we were kids."

"This isn't a game. One person is already dead."

I cocked my head. "Last night you didn't seem so opposed to the idea."

"What did I say to give you that idea?"

"You said it was dangerous, but didn't say anything about not snooping, then when you walked me home, you said you didn't want me out alone after dark if I was going to investigate. Which was very sweet by the way, but not necessary." I got to my feet and headed for the still open front door. "Now, I've work to do, as in bushes to trim and flowers to plant."

He made a sound suspiciously like a growl deep in his throat. "Last night, I thought you were just talking. I didn't think you were serious."

"Serious about what?" Officer Lawrence, and his silent partner, strolled up the walk.

"What I plan on working on today."

He stared silently at me for a moment. "Do you own a pair of gardening gloves, Miss Hart?"

"Of course, I do."

"Could you describe them to me?"

"I can show you." Since I had yet to move my tools to the gardening shed, they were piled in a corner of my living area. I pulled out a pair of fluorescent pink gloves with yellow flowers and another pair of a bright blue with multi-colored butterflies. "These are mine." I waved them at him in a manner resembling someone challenging another to a duel.

"Have you ever seen these?" He pulled a baggy from his pocket that contained a tan and brown glove.

"No, and I would never wear those. They're hideous. Just because a girl is working doesn't mean she can't be pretty while doing so." I grimaced at the ugly things in the bag. "Those look like men's construction…gloves." Something Heath might wear. I fought not to look at him.

"Those are mine," Heath said. "I misplaced them last week."

Officer Lawrence narrowed his eyes. "They were found under the victim's body. According to the coroner's report, the victim also had poison in her stomach. Not only were her dentures covered in the stuff, but she'd ingested some. Forcibly if the bruises on her shoulders were any indication. I do hope you plan on sticking around, Mr. McLeroy."

"You think I killed Maybelle?" Heath paled.

"Just a person of interest, sir. Ma'am." He turned to go.

"Wait. Does that mean I'm off the hook?" I trotted after him.

"For now, Miss Hart." He increased his pace and disappeared around the corner of the common building.

Heath looked a bit shell-shocked when I returned. "I can't believe he thinks I committed murder."

"In his defense, he also suspected me." It was easy to be charitable when I wasn't the one under the microscope. "Keep your chin up. I'm sure if he knew you, he wouldn't suspect you of such a thing." Or would he? I didn't know Heath as much more than a handsome face. Maybe his nice guy routine was a farce so he could prey on elderly women. I gave him a sharp gaze and a wide berth as I went to gather my tools.

"What?" He turned to follow me.

"Nothing."

"You agree with Lawrence!"

"I didn't say that." I eyed the shears in my bucket. They would make a nice weapon should I need one.

"I cannot believe this." He whirled and marched away, leaving me feeling relieved and a bit guilty.

I thought of myself as a good judge of character, normally. My instincts told me that Heath wasn't a killer. Still, a girl couldn't be too careful. I hefted my bucket of tools with brightly colored handles and set off for the greenhouse and the little tool shed that sat at one end of it. Finally, no yellow tape fluttered outside the glass building. I could make myself at home.

After stowing my tools in the wood shed, I stood outside the greenhouse staring at the door. I had tons of work to do inside, but couldn't bring myself to enter.

"What are you doing?" Grandma stepped beside me, eating a banana. "You missed breakfast."

"Did I?" Great. My skinny body couldn't afford to miss a meal.

"I brought you an apple, a blueberry muffin, and one of those little cartons of orange juice." She pulled them from the giant cranberry red bag she carried. "Aren't you going inside?"

"I should." I took the food from her and bit into the apple. "Thanks."

"Come on." She pulled open the door and shoved me in.

I froze. I wasn't sure what I expected, but there was no sign anything horrible had happened there, other than a few days lack of water to wilt some of the plants. Even the box of rat poison was gone. It was as if Maybelle had never been there.

Grandma followed and sighed. "I was hoping for a little something."

I chose to ignore her statement and filled a watering can at a nearby spigot. Then, watching her from the corner of my eye and hoping she didn't hurt anything, I watered my plants. Something crashed behind me. I whirled.

"Seriously?" I had no idea what my gardening budget was, but I doubted I had enough to replace a four foot ceramic pot. "Grandma, please be careful."

"It was ugly anyway. All I did was drag this shovel from under that counter. I can't help it if I broke something behind me." She peered closer at the shovel.

"What is this white powder stuff?"

"Where did you get that?" I took the shovel from her.

"It was under there behind some boxes. Is that poison? Wouldn't the police have taken it?"

"I think its fertilizer." I peered under the counter. Someone had been digging in my greenhouse.

A loud knocking ensued overhead. I misjudged the height of the counter and banged my head backing out. "Ow!" I touched the tender spot and glanced up.

Heath straddled a thick branch while sawing the limb of another. He caught me looking and glared.

"What's the matter with Handsome?" Grandma tossed her banana peel into a trashcan.

"The police think he killed Maybelle and when he asked me if I believed them, I hesitated in answering."

"Hmm. He doesn't look like a killer."

He stared at us for a moment, then resumed sawing.

"Heath!" Alice stood, hands on hips, under the tree. "That can wait. I need you to move something." When he didn't respond, she picked up a twig and slapped his foot.

He yelled and fell sideways. As he grappled for a foothold, the branch he'd been sawing broke and crashed through the top of the greenhouse. Seconds later, Heath followed and landed on his back in my tomato plants. Red juice oozed from under him.

Grandma gagged and clapped a hand over her mouth. "Is he dead?"

"Heath." I shook him.

"Don't touch me. I'm covered in glass. Get that idiot manager in here."

I ignored his don't touch me and grabbed his hand, pulling him to a sitting position. "Let me check your back."

"I'm fine." A cut over his eye bled. "Thank goodness the branch broke the glass ceiling before I did. You!" He pointed at Alice. "What were you thinking?"

"I'm sorry. I needed your attention."

"For what?" he growled.

"I need you to move Maybelle's things out of her cottage so I can move someone else in."

"It doesn't look as if anything is badly damaged except my tomatoes." I swiped a rag at Heath's back. "You might want to change first." I glanced at my busted ceiling. "And call a repairman."

"Alice can call the repairman while I change my clothes." Heath limped from the building.

"Should I call a doctor?" Alice chewed a manicured nail.

"No." I stared after him. "Just call someone to repair the greenhouse. Heath will be fine once he cleans his minor cuts. If not, he's a big boy and will call a doctor himself." Someone could have easily been killed by the falling branch or broken glass. Heath could have broken his neck. If he died, would that be justice for Maybelle or the end of another innocent person?

6

I didn't see Heath again for a couple of hours when I caught sight of him hobbling toward lunch while on crutches. I hurried to catch up. "You hurt yourself?"

He glared. "I did fall out of a tree, Shelby, and crashed through a glass roof. Of course I hurt myself. Sprained my knee and suffered minor lacerations."

"I'm sorry. I didn't think it was serious. You walked away."

"Really? How else was I supposed to get to the doctor?" He stopped and faced me. "Are you sorry enough to help me clear my name now that you're no longer a suspect?"

"Oh, well, sure." With Cheryl coming to help me, I'd continue searching for Maybelle's killer, even if Heath turned out to be the guilty party. I'd heard of bad guys pretending to help to throw suspicion off themselves.

He made a disgusted sound in his throat and

reached for the dining room door. "You still think I might have killed Maybelle."

"I didn't say that." I opened the door for him.

"You didn't have to." Once inside, he transferred his sour mood to Alice. "This is your fault."

"I'm sorry." Tears welled in her eyes. "I didn't think a simple pat on the foot would cause you to fall or I would not have done it. How long will you be out of work?"

Heath groaned and lowered himself into a chair. "Maybe a week, and a whack with a stick as big as your wrist was hardly a simple pat."

"Oh, dear. Well, Shelby will have to take up the slack."

"Seriously? Have you looked at me? How do you propose I move furniture?" I planted fists on my skinny hips. Had the woman lost her mind? "Perhaps you could hire someone from a temporary agency?"

"Great idea!" Alice clapped her hands. "Take care of that for me." She whirled and clomped away.

Someone really needed to teach that woman how to walk in high heels. "Doesn't she realize I have enough work to do?" I sighed and turned to Heath. "What would you like to eat?"

"A little bit of anything that looks good. Thanks." He leaned his crutches against the chair next to him.

Obviously his injury hadn't affected his appetite. I grabbed two plates and got in line behind a couple of women I hadn't met yet. There had to be a way for me to meet all the residents. Perhaps an ice cream social? A place where mingling wouldn't seem out of place.

"Oh, Myrna. Maybelle was harmless." A silver haired lady used tongs to pluck a couple of slices of ham from the platter.

"Maybe not. What if losing her teeth was nothing more than a ploy to be nosy?"

"What are you worried about? It's not like you have any secrets."

"You'd be surprised what secrets I have!" Myrna stomped her foot and bypassed the other lady in line.

"For Pete's sake." Her left-behind friend shook her head. "I doubt she's hiding anything important enough to kill over." She took her plate and headed for a nearby table.

Interesting. I filled mine and Heath's plates with fixings to make sandwiches, grabbed single serving bags of chips and headed back to join him. "What is Myrna's last name?" I asked, setting his plate in front of him.

"Smith. Why?" He lifted the top of his bun and frowned. "No mustard?"

I tossed him a packet from the basket on the table. "Who is the woman to your right with the silver hair? Don't look!" I said as he turned his head.

"Then how am I supposed to know who you're talking about? That's Ann Wilson."

I spread mayonnaise on the top bun of my roll. "If you were to suspect someone in Shady Acres of being capable of murder, who would it be?"

"Hmm." He glanced around the room. "Bob Satchett is a bit of a hot head. Came here about six months ago. Keeps to himself. Then, there's Harry Weasley. He doesn't talk to anyone, attend any functions, nothing. The only time you see him outside his cottage is at meal times."

"He looks a bit like Mr. Toad." I clapped a hand

over my mouth. “That was not nice.”

“Apt description.” He bit into his sandwich. After swallowing, he continued, “I don’t think you should take my word for things, though. I don’t get along with Bob, so I might be a bit biased, and I know little to nothing about Harry. You need to find a way to question these people.”

“Maybe I should just come right out and ask them if they murdered Maybelle and see how they react.” I was about to that point. The poor woman had been dead for almost three days and I knew nothing, and doubted the police knew much more. Her death might go unavenged.

Speaking of the police… Officer Lawrence appeared in the doorway, scanned the room, and made a beeline for my grandmother’s table. He pulled out a chair and sat down. Seconds later, Grandma’s giggles reached my ears. Surely, the officer wasn’t here on a social call?

Wait. If Grandma could get into his good graces, she might be able to siphon information. Lots of things were discovered over pillow talk, or forms of talking thereof.

After lunch, I cleared mine and Heath’s plate and headed for the manager’s office to use Alice’s phone to call a temporary service. I didn’t have my laptop and WiFi set up yet and had no way of finding phone numbers. If Alice wanted me to do her job, then I’d use her office.

I knocked on the door in the main building that said ‘Manager’ and entered when no one said anything. I sat at her cherry wood desk and ran my hands over the polished wood, noting that I was in desperate need of a manicure. I turned on her computer. Of course, it was password protected. I chewed the inside of my lip. If I couldn't get into her computer, then I definitely needed the WiFi password so I could set up my laptop in my cottage.

I shuffled through the pile of papers on her desk. Nothing but resident registrations and background checks. I stopped at Harry Weasley's. It said he had taught fifth grade social studies at Cooper Elementary. The very same school I once taught at. I would have to check on that.

"Find what you were looking for?" Alice stood in the doorway, arms crossed. "If you're going to snoop, you should have at least closed the door."

"I wasn't snooping. I was hoping to use your computer to find the number for a temp agency. Since that is out of the question, I need the WiFi password." I stood, sliding Harry's form back into the stack of papers.

"You still haven't read the papers I gave you. All the information you need is in there." Alice shoved me away from her desk. She scribbled something on a post-it note. "The password." She then typed her password into her computer and turned the screen to face me. "At your service."

"I've read most of the papers, but you keep adding to my work load. I'm exhausted when I get off work." I found a number for a temporary service, wrote it on a post-it, and headed outside. I pulled out my cell phone and within three minutes had a promise for a general handyman to arrive at the retirement community by eight o'clock in the morning.

I headed for the shed and grabbed my shears and a

large wicker basket. I had to get some work done before Cheryl showed up or Alice complained. First on the list were the rose bushes.

Several bushes later, my legs sported a few scratches, perspiration dotted my upper lip, and I couldn't remember the last time I was happier. I sat on a nearby bench and guzzled from a water bottle. When I'd finished, I set the bottle on the edge of the bench and bent to retrieve my tools from where I'd set them.

What? I plucked the top part of a set of dentures from the dirt. A little more digging revealed the bottom half. Maybelle's teeth? If not, whose? And if they are hers, who did the ones in her mouth when she died belong to?

Grandma and Officer Lawrence stood by the gazebo. He leaned forward and whispered something in her ear. My heart stopped when I thought he would kiss her. I shuddered, relieved when he smiled and turned away. He headed down the path toward me.

"Here." I held the teeth by my fingertips. "I found these. They might be Maybelle's."

His brows drew together. "Her's were in her mouth."

"Were they?" I wiggled my eyebrows. "What if those weren't hers?"

"Why wouldn't they be? That would be stranger than…well, anything I've ever seen."

"I know I have an over-active imagination," I said, "but what if…Maybelle wasn't the intended victim? Huh? What if those teeth belong to someone else and she thought they were hers. They seemed large for her mouth."

He held out a baggie he'd pulled from his pocket.

"A simple DNA test will show us." After I dropped the teeth in, he shoved the bag into his pocket. "You're a strange one, Shelby Hart." He marched down the path and out the gate.

I cupped my hands around my mouth. "You're welcome!"

He lifted a hand without looking back.

"Isn't he divine?" Grandma hugged my arm. "I think I'm going to marry him."

"Did he ask?" I looked at her in alarm.

"No, but he will. I'll make sure of it. Oh, look, there's Cheryl. Yoohoo!" She jumped up and down waving her arms.

"Stop before you break something." I put a hand on her arm to restrain her.

"Grandma!" Cheryl, almost six feet tall, curvaceous in all the right places, brunette and beautiful, rushed toward us pulling a rolling suitcase. "I'm yours for one whole week."

"Good." Grandma hugged her. "You can help Shelby catch an old woman's killer. She's getting nowhere by herself."

I rolled my eyes and made the hug a group one. "I'm making tiny progress. The cops don't have anything either, which reminds me..." I gave Grandma a serious look. "Since you're so cozy with Officer Lawrence, I want you drilling him—"

"Naughty girl." Grandma waved her finger.

"What? No. Gross. Drilling him for information. Gee whiz, Grandma." I put my hands to my flaming cheeks, no doubt leaving behind dirty handprints. I needed a shower. Not only to wash away the grime of my job but to wash away the mental picture my grandmother left in my head.

Cheryl laughed. "This place is beautiful. Cottages for the residents. Flagstone walks. Must be expensive."

"It is." Grandma linked her arms with us. "But worth every penny. We don't need to cook or clean. That's all taken care of for us. Plus, we have a handsome handyman, but I think Shelby has dibs on him."

"No, I don't. I'm not interested in romance." I glanced at Cheryl and shook my head.

"Probably for the best," Grandma said. "After Donald dumping you, why you'll need time to heal. Bless your heart."

I slipped my arm free from Grandma's hold. "I have to put these tools away. I'll meet you at the cottage. I'm sure Grandma has a key."

"You bet I do!"

I had no privacy with her here. None. Nada. Zilch. Still, I liked having her close. I wouldn't mind Mom being closer, but at the age of fifty she'd be insulted, not to mention she wasn't old enough for Shady Acres. Now, if a job became available that I could get her interested in… It was something to keep in mind.

I stowed my tools in the shed and peeled off my gloves. I started to leave when I noticed the larger pair of shears that I would use when trimming trees was not where I'd left it. Instead of hanging on a hook, safely out of reach, it was stuck in the dirt. Over one of the handles was one of my extra gloves.

It almost seemed as if the glove waved a warning at me.

7

"This is a really cute place." Cheryl set her bags in the guest room, then turned to me with a concerned look. "How are you doing after the whole Donald thing? He struts around school like a proud peacock."

"Great. I like the job, I'm making friends, and gardening is therapeutic. How is the jerk, anyway, other than self-absorbed?"

Cheryl plopped onto the sofa and, crossing her feet at the ankles, propped them on the glass-topped coffee table. "Still a jerk and dating the teacher who took over your class. Sorry. The good news is there have been so many complaints about him from parents and staff that there are rumors he may soon be moved elsewhere."

I hated to think ill of anyone, but knowing he might be given the boot filled me with no small amount of pleasure. "You've been there a long time. Have you ever heard of a Harry Weasley? He would be retired now."

"No, at least not in the last six years. Why?"

"Just wondering." I moved to the kitchen to grab a couple of diet sodas. "Everyone eats at assigned mealtimes here, unless you cook for yourself in your cottage. I still have to work while you're here, and there's a social mingle with finger foods tomorrow night. It might be a good time for us to do some nosing around."

"No suspects?"

"I was the primary, but now that honor has gone to the handyman, Heath McLeroy. They found his glove under the body."

"Do you think he did it?"

"No." I might have hesitated in answering when Heath asked, but deep down, I didn't think him capable of such an act.

"I want to meet this handyman." Cheryl smiled as I handed her a glass of soda.

"Why?"

"Because your voice got all warm and fuzzy when you said his name."

"Ridiculous." My face heated. "I've sworn off men and romance."

"Sure you have. So, what's first on our agenda for snooping?"

"It'll be supper soon. You can help me keep an eye and ear open for any mention of Maybelle." I sipped my soda. "Without asking questions outright, I'm not sure we'll find out anything."

"Then we ask outright. If someone mentions her name, I'll act like the curious visitor who wants the scoop. What's the worst they can do? Clam up?" She set her glass on the table and swung her legs to the floor. Her nice, shapely legs.

I glanced at my pencil thin ones. "Let me shower and change, then I'll be ready to head over."

In the master bath, I turned the shower to hot and dropped my clothes. While I knew I shouldn't compare myself to others, I couldn't stop from studying my body in the mirror. Small breasts, tiny waist, slim hips and skinny legs. Not even close to the curves Cheryl had. Top it off with a head of curly hair that didn't behave and it was no wonder Donald broke off our wedding. He wanted a trophy wife. I was more like a trophy teenager. I leaned and peered at a spot on my face. Was that a zit under the dirt? Ugh. Just proved my point that I was a twenty-eight-year-old teenager.

After my shower, I donned a summer dress with stripes and flowers, matching sandals, forgoing the rain boots for an hour or two, and joined Cheryl in the living room. She'd changed, too, into formfitting capris and a rib hugging blouse. "I hate you," I said, grabbing my house key from the dinette table.

"What did I do?" Cheryl frowned.

"Look at you and look at me."

She narrowed her eyes. "You look cute."

"Great. Thanks." I stormed out of the cottage.

"What?"

I whirled. "You're beautiful in anything you put on, despite your height. How many women can pull that off? Me…I'm cute. Like a little girl."

She covered her mouth with one hand and burst into laughter. "You have no idea how beautiful you are. Like a mischievous fairy from the forest. Tiny, mighty, and gorgeous. You ooze femininity."

"You're just saying that." My insides warmed.

"Why else would Donald almost marry you? Don't you notice how heads turn when you enter a room?"

"I've noticed how they turn when you do."

"I'm an Amazon. Do you know how hard it is to find a man taller than me? Stop being silly and let's go eat." She put an arm around my shoulders. "Introduce me to this handyman that makes your eyes sparkle."

"That's him on the crutches." I rushed forward to open the door for Heath.

"Who's the gorgeous giant?" He motioned over his shoulder at Cheryl.

"My best friend, Cheryl Leroix." Just like that the warm feeling over Cheryl's admiring words flew away. And, to make things worse, Heath was a few inches over six feet. Plenty tall enough to catch Cheryl's eye.

The three of us chose a table away from the other staff. April glared our way but didn't say anything. How many people did she think she could shove around a table for ten anyway?

"Who's the woman giving us the stink eye?" Cheryl asked, choosing a seat on the opposite side of me.

"That's the manager, Alice. She's a bit bi-polar." I quickly pointed out the names I did know. "The best place to listen to gossip is in the food line."

"The best way to do that is to browse the food, stepping in and out of line in pretense of seeing what they have to offer. I'll be right back." She darted for the buffet line.

"She's going to set most of these old geezers' heart into A-fib," Heath said.

"Yeah, she affects Junior High boys that way, too. It looks like there's a choice of beef or chicken enchiladas. A Mexican food buffet. Which do you want?"

He put his hand over mine, sending shock waves up my arm. "You're a true friend, Shelby. I appreciate your help while I'm on these crutches, and not only with getting my meals."

"That's why Cheryl's here. To help me find out what happened to Maybelle." I slipped my hand free and headed for the end of the line.

Cheryl stopped weaving in and out and joined me. "See that man? The one who looked as if he just sucked a lemon? He yelled at me to get my giant arse out of his way."

"That would be Bob Satchett. Did you learn anything?"

"Only that Maybelle was considered not quite right in the head and folks were getting tired of humoring her odd behavior. Anyone of these people could have killed her. They aren't infirm, seem in reasonably good health for their age, and active. It wouldn't be hard for them to slip poison into something."

"That's what I thought." I pointed out Harry Weasley. "There's the man who said he retired from Cooper Elementary."

"I've never seen him before in my life, but I can call the secretary and have her check the files." She pulled her cell phone from the pocket of her pants and typed in a note.

It was going to be a good thing to have Cheryl here helping me. Two heads were better than one and all that. Now, to solve Maybelle's murder within a week's time.

Loaded down with my plate and Heath's, making

sure I gave him twice the amount I took for myself, I headed back to the table, surprised to see Grandma and Mom both sitting there. “Mom!” I set the plates down and kissed her cheek.

“I came for dinner and to check on you and your grandmother. You look cute, dear.”

I cringed, but kept my smile in place. “It’s great to see you. I’m going to try and get you a job here so you can live with us.”

“No, I like my house, thank you.” She scowled. Her face brightened when Cheryl joined us. “Don’t you look pretty? What a nice surprise.”

“Hey, Mrs. H.” Shelby sat next to Grandma. “How do you like hanging with the old folks?”

“Who says we’re old?”

Cheryl cast me an amused glance. “I’m here to help Shelby catch a killer. Want to make it a three-some?”

“I’m already working on it. I have a wine date with Officer Lawrence in an hour.” Grandma wiggled her penciled on eyebrows. “I’ll get information out of that man one way or the other.”

“Good. I need my name cleared.” Heath bit into a taco. “Anyone could have gotten my work gloves. The lock on the shed had rusted through. I replaced it the morning Shelby stumbled across Maybelle.”

“The temporary handyman will be here in the morning. You’ll need to hobble around and show him the ropes,” I said with a grin.

“That’s cruel, Shelby.” Mom gave me ‘the look’. “I taught you better than that.”

“He almost fell on me, Mom.”

“I did not.” Heath finished off the taco and reached

for a taquito. “If not for Alice, I would have remained safely in the tree, and unless you were sitting in the tomatoes, you were in no danger of being landed on.”

“This week is going to be a blast.” Cheryl cut into a Chimichanga. “Mealtimes alone are more entertaining than the teacher’s lounge during a cat fight.”

A commotion behind me had us all turning in our seats. Bob and Harold, the Belcher, were toe-to-toe, faces red, yelling at each other. Alice’s vain attempts to separate them did no good.

“I’ll handle this.” Cheryl rose to her full height, adopted her teacher’s look, and approached the two men. Grabbing each by an ear, she pulled them apart as I rushed up. “What is this meaning of two grown men acting like children in public?” Cheryl looked from one to the other.

“He accused me of riffling through his cottage.” Harold crossed his arms. “I am not a sneak or a thief.”

“Well, somebody was in there that shouldn’t have been.”

Bob’s face was so red, I almost feared for his health.

“You live right next door to me. Maybelle isn’t here, so you’re the next logical choice.”

“Mr. Satchett,” I motioned for Cheryl to release them. “Isn’t it possible housecleaning moved something? Is anything missing?”

“Not missing, just moved.”

“Then, there you go.” I gave a reassuring smile, the same kind I would have given quarrelling eight year olds.

“Just watch yourself, Harold.” Bob leaned in. “We all know what happens to those who stick their nose in other people's business. It's bound to get chopped off!" He stormed from the dining room, leaving the place in stunned silence.

A few seconds later the place roared with conversation. Harold glanced around, then headed outside.

"That was fun." Cheryl grinned and returned to her meal.

"Amazing the way you handled them." Heath gave an appreciative grin. "I'm glad you weren't my teacher."

I squelched down a bit of jealousy. I could have stopped their argument, maybe, somehow. I focused on my food and let the others continue the conversation without me.

I really didn't know why I was acting like a petulant child. Jealousy wasn't a trait that visited often. Still, the way my new friends and family fawned over Cheryl grated a bit. All through childhood we'd been teased about our differences in appearance. That was what brought us together as friends. So why the sour grapes?

Because I wanted to prove I could excel at something. I'd failed getting married to Donald, hadn't enjoyed teaching as much as I'd thought I would, and still couldn't be independent with Grandma following me everywhere. Succeeding at my job here at Shady Acres and, possibly, forming a close friendship with Heath, would be a big step toward re-establishing my self-esteem.

I had to solve Maybelle's murder. I just had to. If I did, I'd have proven myself in a big way and cleared Heath's name in the process.

8

The next morning, I waited just inside the glass doors leading to the lobby for our substitute handyman to arrive. I'd promised Heath I'd bring the man to the dining room. So far, he was fifteen minutes late. That act did not instill a lot of confidence.

A forest-green pickup truck roared into the driveway. A man in coveralls and a white tee shirt climbed out. He sauntered toward the building, wiping his bald head with a red, white, and blue bandana. He yanked open the door, his steps faltering when he saw me.

"Miss Hart? Got a flat. Sorry." He held out a blackened hand.

"Dave Mason?" I shook his dirty hand, then wiped it on my jeans. "Follow me and I'll introduce you to the man whose job you'll do for the next week or so."

"Wonderful, but I got to tell you I can't do any heavy lifting."

I stopped. "Excuse me? That's what I requested. I need someone to do the heavy work." Alice was going to have a conniption fit.

"Bad back. I can do lawn work just fine."

"But, that's my job."

He raked his gaze over me. "I reckon you aren't much good at heavy work. Too small."

I supposed I could get Cheryl to help me…wait a minute! I needed to assert myself. "Mr. Mason. If you cannot do the work I hired you to do, then I'll have to insist you leave."

"Don't be hasty, little lady. I'll do the work."

"Wonderful." I marched toward the dining room and left the man under Heath's supervision.

Cheryl and Grandma were still having breakfast. I told them I'd be in the greenhouse working and to come fetch me when, and if, they found something for us to investigate. I think Grandma took that as a personal challenge since she bolted from her seat and began questioning the other residents. I shook my head and headed to work.

Not only did I have some weeding to do in the herb garden, and watering of the plants in the greenhouse, I needed to somehow put plastic over the hole in the roof until a repairman came out. I wasn't sure what was taking Alice so long. I thought for sure she would have called straightaway. Then, once that was finished, I needed to make sure everything was in order for the social that evening. Perhaps a record player with songs from the time the residents were young. I could make an announcement for everyone to come dressed when they felt their finest.

I pulled out my cell phone, ran the idea past Alice,

who loved it, and asked her to make the announcement then call the repairman. Seconds later, the announcement came over the loud speaker. One job complete.

I stepped into the greenhouse. Birdie dug in the dirt under the counter where Maybelle had lain. "Birdie?"

"You're taking too long, Missy. I thought I'd do some digging of my own."

"What do you expect to find?"

She crawled out. "I have no idea." Tears welled in her eyes. "Life goes on as if she never existed."

I put my arms around her. "Maybelle is missed, honey."

"No, she isn't. She was a difficult, nosy, prickly woman, but she was my friend." She wiped her nose on her sleeve. "I want to see justice done."

So did I. "Want to help me put plastic on the roof? You can hold the ladder. It might help take your mind off things."

"I don't see what good I am, but I suppose I can hold a ladder."

I retrieved the ladder from against the building and stood it up. "Don't let me fall."

"No guarantees."

With my heart in my throat, I climbed the ladder. I probably should have asked the new guy, but he'd be plenty busy doing all the things Heath wasn't able to get to. The ladder shook under me. I glanced down to see Birdie leaning against it eating a cookie. "Birdie!"

"Oh, sorry. I missed breakfast." She put both hands back on the ladder.

"Hand me an edge of that plastic roll and the duct tape. Slowly, please, and one at a time."

She handed me the tape and I set it on the top step of the twenty-four foot ladder. Then, slowly but surely, I began taping the plastic over the hole.

"Shelby Marie Hart!"

I turned, missing the rung. As the ladder fell, I jumped to the nearest shelf and smashed a fern. "Grandma! Are you trying to kill me?"

"What are you doing on that ladder?"

"Fixing the roof. Temporarily, of course." I jumped to the ground and tried to prop up the leaves of the mangled plant I'd landed on. Maybe I'd have Mr. Mason finish the roof job.

"Have Cheryl get up there. She won't have to go as high." Grandma crossed her thin arms and glared. "You can't get killed. We need you to help solve this murder."

"That's what I've been telling her," Birdie said, wiping the cookie crumbs from her hands.

"Did you learn anything from Officer Lawrence last night?"

Grandma motioned her head toward Birdie. "Oh, I learned a lot, but nothing I can talk about in polite company."

"Gross." I shuddered.

"I'm leaving!" Birdie threw up her hands and stalked away.

"While the two of you talk, I'll finish this poor attempt at roof repair." Cheryl climbed up the ladder.

"Did you learn anything about the case or not?" I gave up on the poor fern. It would either revive or become compost in the next day or two.

"That man is as tight-lipped as a clam, but I did do some snooping when he went to the bathroom."

That could get her arrested and thrown behind bars. "You can't be doing that. What if he would have caught you?"

She shrugged. "I would have charmed my way free. Do you want to know what I found out or not?"

"Of course, I do."

"Maybelle has a rap sheet." Grandma pretended to study her manicure, but stared up at me from lowered lashes.

"Stop playing around and tell me." I stomped my foot.

"Petty theft, that kind of thing. A couple of parking tickets." She leaned against the counter. "Mr. Lawrence had a file on his coffee table."

"He left it in the open?"

"Not really. I had to move several books and magazines to find it. Here's the thing." She held up her hand. "If Maybelle wasn't such a nice girl, it's very possible she was involved in something she shouldn't have been and was killed for it. We need to search her things. Have they cleared out her cottage yet?"

I shook my head. "That's scheduled for tomorrow, I think."

Cheryl jumped from the ladder. "What are we waiting for? Let's go."

I locked the greenhouse and led them to Maybelle's former home. The door was locked. I stepped back, looking for an open window.

"Let me." Grandma shouldered me out of the way and pulled a lock picking kit from her purse. "I came prepared."

I did not want to know how she came about this particular skill. Seconds later, we were in the messiest home I'd ever stepped foot into. Clothes and dirty dishes covered every available surface. Books and magazines were strewn on the floor. "Someone has already ransacked the place."

"I think this is how she lived," Cheryl said. "I pity the girls in housekeeping."

"Start digging. There has to be something buried in here." Grandma headed for the kitchen.

"I'll take the master bedroom," I said, hoping I didn't uncover something dead.

The bedroom was worse than the front room. I shoved a pile of clothing aside with my foot and moved to the dresser. A wooden box, the type men kept their doo dads in, set on top. Using my fingernail, I lifted the lid. Inside were watches and cufflinks. Had she stolen the entire thing or collected the men's items over a period of time? Question two…why hadn't the police taken the box? I shrugged. Maybe no one had reported anything missing at Shady Acres. She could have brought the box with her.

I opened the top drawer, caught sight of plain white underwear, and slammed the drawer closed. On second thought, I opened it again. Women who wanted to hide something often stuck it in their underwear drawer.

Bingo! I pulled out a Manilla envelope. Inside were several photographs. At first glance, they seemed to be of Shady Acre residents. I set the envelope aside and moved to the next drawer. Nothing interesting in the next two so I checked under the mattress then went to the closet.

Heavens to Betsy, how did anyone put another item of clothing in the jammed space? I glanced at the top shelf. Several boxes, tossed in haphazardly, seemed ready to fall. The first box I pulled down contained a Glock nine millimeter with a cute pink handle. Why hadn't the police taken it? I closed the box and left the gun alone. Maybe since it didn't pertain to Maybelle's death, they left it with her personal items. The other boxes contained years and years of receipts. No help there.

Next, I glanced under the bed. Way too crammed to find anything, then headed to the master bathroom. I stared at the cluttered countertop, then opened the medicine cabinet. Assorted prescriptions for pain and anxiety filled the inside. Poor Maybelle seemed to suffer from more than kleptomania. Wait. Those weren't her name on the bottles. I read Birdie's name, Harry Weasley's on one of the anxiety meds, even Bob Satchett's name was there.

"Find anything?" Cheryl walked up behind me.

"She might very well have been a drug addict, stealing prescriptions from the other residents to feed her habit." I closed the cabinet. "Does no one lock their doors around here?"

"Maybe she got a hold of a master key."

"Good point. I'll ask Alice if one was ever noticed missing." I grabbed the envelope from the bed and headed to the front room. "Grandma? Find anything?"

She waved a sheet of paper. "She kept a schedule of the residents."

"That would make sense, since she was stealing from them." I dumped the contents of the envelope on the table after knocking several books to the floor. "She was also photographing everyone."

"Our little Maybelle was not only a kook, but a thief."

"Maybe the absent-mindedness was a ploy so people wouldn't take too long of a look at her. It would be the perfect disguise."

Grandma tapped a photo of Alice with her nail. "These don't seem to be about the residents going about their lives. They seem to be more like spying. Alice is unlocking the door to a cottage that isn't hers. Weasley is watching Bob and Myrna Smith. Here's one of Heath entering Alice's office. Was she stealing, gathering information, or both?"

"That's what we need to find out." I stuffed the photos back in the envelope, added the schedule, and slid them into Grandma's purse.

"Holy cow." Heath peered into the cottage. "I think Alice needs to hire a crew to clean this out. It's too much for Amber and Becky. What are y'all doing in here?"

"Snoo—just checking on some things," Grandma said, spotting Dave. "Getting a grasp of the work that needs to be done. Have fun." She grabbed my arm, and leaving Cheryl to follow, pushed our way out of the cottage. "That was close. Who is that man in overalls? I almost spilled the beans to a stranger."

"The substitute handyman." I glanced over our shoulder. Heath and Dave looked our way. "We could have been caught by more than just them. What if Alice would have seen us?"

"I would have thought of something."

"I'd like to know what you were doing in the victim's cottage." Officer Lawrence stepped from behind a tree. "Care to share any information?"

Grandma fiddled with a button on his shirt. "We would if we'd found out anything. Didn't the police search her place?"

"A bit. But since it isn't a crime scene—" He removed Grandma's hand. "Ladies, I'll tell you this one time only. Do not interfere in my investigation." He turned and marched toward Maybelle's cottage.

9

*D*ressed in a vintage flapper dress, I stood next to Cheryl, who wore a formal gown from modern day because of her size, and Grandma in a red flapper dress to compliment my black one. Grandma and I made petite bookends to Cheryl, but the three of us stood in the doorway and surveyed the crowd of residents in every type of clothing imaginable. We had pimp suits, tuxedos, formal gowns, a fifties prom dress…you name it, we had it. Heath wore something Gatsby might have worn and looked quite dashing, even with the crutches.

"Remember…we are here to mingle and question the people in those photos," I told my companions. "We'll congregate in my cottage after the social."

"We can have a bit of fun." Grandma pulled one of those long cigarette holders they used to use back in the day.

"You can't smoke in here." I wasn't aware she smoked.

"I'm not going to light it, silly. It's for allure." With her head high, Grandma sashayed into the crowd.

I shrugged and headed for the table where Heath and Dave, still in his coveralls, sat. "How did the first day go?"

"Just great." Dave stuffed half a cupcake in his mouth.

Heath rolled his eyes, but kept his mouth shut. "We have some, uh, heavier items that need to be moved. Do you think your Amazon friend can help out?"

"I'll ask her, but she isn't here to work. She's on vacation." I knew that substitute wasn't going to work out. I should have given him the boot that morning. "Dave, we had this discussion. Either you do the work or—"

Yelling from the corner drew my attention. Birdie and Bob hurled insults at each other until Birdie clasped a hand to her chest and sagged into a chair.

I rushed to her side. "Do I need to call an ambulance?"

"She's faking it," Bob said with a scowl. "Ain't nothing wrong with that biddie."

Birdie's eyes flashed, confirming his words. "I had a twinge, Bob. You can't say I didn't. Not with any certainty. If you don't stop accusing me of taking your watch I might have a heart attack for real."

"You were seen snooping around my cottage."

"No one in their right mind would go near that pig sty." She pushed to her feet, every pink curl on her head quivering with indignation.

I couldn't help but wonder whether Bob's watch was one of those in Maybelle's box. I made a mental note to let Officer Lawrence know. "Why don't the two of you head to opposite sides of the room and take a break?"

Bob seemed taken aback. "Why? We came here together."

"Yeah, Shelby." Birdie slipped her arm in his. "We're on a date."

For Pete's sake. I shook my head and took my own advice.

Harold Ball belched loud enough to deter me from my original destination and sent me to the opposite corner of the room where Mr. Weasley was stuffing finger sandwiches into every available pocket. From a few feet over, Alice waved her hand wildly in a gesture telling me to make him stop. I nodded.

"Mr. Weasley."

"Harry, please." He peered up at me from behind thick glasses which distorted his eyes so badly it was hard to tell his expression.

"Well, then, Harry, I must insist you stop filching the food. If you continue, there won't be enough for everyone else."

"I get hungry."

"We all do. Perhaps you could keep food in the refrigerator in your room?"

"Perhaps." He unloaded his pockets, leaving the sandwiches in a pile on the starched white tablecloth. "I'll go find me a woman to dance with."

A big band number played from the record player. It was all I could do to keep my feet from tapping along. If I hadn't received a stern warning from Alice that I was not at the functions to participate, but to make sure everyone was having a good time, the only person I would want to dance with was Heath and he was out of commission. Still, I had a tiny regret over taking a job that sometimes had me working sixteen hour days. At the age of twenty-eight, I liked to think I had a lot of fun left in me.

Heath waved me over the moment Dave left the table. "You've got to fire him."

"I know." I fell into a chair.

"We have to help the girls clean out Maybelle's cottage for a new renter and he's worthless. He'll fill a grocery size bag and carry out just that one bag. I carry more than that on these things." He slapped his crutches.

"Did you see a wooden box full of men's watches and things?"

He sighed. "Are you feeling sorry for me in the slightest?"

I grinned. "A bit." I patted his cheek. "You poor thing. Now, did you?"

"Yeah. We handed it over to Officer Lawrence last night. He seemed interested."

"One of those watches might be Bob Satchette's."

A sharp look from Alice got me to my feet. Maybe Bob could answer some questions for me. He seemed in a much better mood as he laughed at something Birdie said. In the photo Maybelle had of him, he'd seemed cozy with Myrna Smith. Now, that woman glared daggers in his direction.

Before I left, I put a hand on Heath's shoulder. "Maybelle had some photos in her possession. One of them showed you jimmying the lock on Alice's office door. What was up with that?"

He turned, eyes wide. "Why would she have a picture of me?"

I shrugged.

"Alice lost her key. I had to get into the office so she could retrieve her spare. It was innocent, Shelby." His eyes narrowed. "Don't tell me you're starting to believe I killed Maybelle."

"I'm just knocking off leads. Don't get your drawers wadded up." I made my pats a little harder, parting with one final whack, then headed over to talk to Myrna.

I sat in an empty seat at her table. "You don't look as if you're having fun."

"Look at that pink haired hussy."

I glanced to where Bob swept Birdie into a swing dance. "They're good."

"I taught him those moves."

"The rat." If I wanted information from her, I needed to be on her good side. "What happened?"

"It's my fault, really. I knew when I started seeing him, on the sly, of course. I do have a reputation to keep, unlike Birdie. Anyway, I knew he was Shady Acres's Casanova. He keeps Cialis on his nightstand for crying out loud."

Eew. I needed to change the subject, but curiousity welled more than in the proverbial cat. "He didn't like a secret liaison?"

"No. Seems he likes to flaunt his women."

"Was Maybelle ever one of them?"

"I did find her teeth on his nightstand once. Not sure whether he wanted them there or she left them during one of her snooping visits. That woman could get into any locked door. A marvel, really." She stood and patted my hand. "Thanks for talking, but I'm heading over there to get my man back."

That left Bob for me to talk to and he was busy. With two ladies.

Grandma yoo hooed me from across the room. She had a grip on Harold Ball's arm to rival a wrestler. "He has something to tell you!"

I met Cheryl's amused glance. We met halfway across the room and continued to where Grandma was. "I thought we were going to exchange notes later."

"This is important. Tell her, Harold." Grandma gave him a little shove.

"I saw that new guy stick something in his pocket from Maybelle's place."

"Really? What?" I crossed my arms.

"Something from a box in the closet."

"Where is Dave now?"

"Last I saw him, he was whispering with Weasley by the men's room. Can I go now, Ida?"

She kissed his cheek, leaving a red lip print. "Sure you can, honey. Have fun. Poor thing," she said as he left. "Can't quite get over the fact I'm spending time with Officer Lawrence."

"Spare the details unless you get information out of him. I'm going to find Dave."

"I'm going with you." Cheryl marched beside me like a celebrity bodyguard. "What are you going to say when you find him?"

"I'm going to play it by ear. There he is."

Dave sat alone on a bench near the pool. He didn't glance up until we sat next to him.

"What's wrong, Dave?" I really hoped his mood wasn't bad because I planned on firing him in the morning. Laziness and stealing could not be tolerated. Still, I'd feel bad for him.

"Nothing." He forced a grin. "Just enjoying the nice evening."

"Someone saw you take something from the cottage you were cleaning out today. What did you take?"

"Nothing, I swear." He held up his hands. "That person is lying."

"Dave, why would they lie?"

"I have no idea. Why don't you ask them?" He bolted to his feet. "Unless you plan on having me arrested, I'm going to the cottage I'm sharing with Heath." He mumbled something about not getting his own place and shuffled down the walk.

"That's guilty behavior if I ever saw any." Cheryl watched him until he turned the corner. "What did he take?"

"Something from a shoebox in the closet. It would have to be small. Paper perhaps."

"Let's go see if the boxes are still there."

We hurried to Maybelle's cottage. The door was locked, the shades drawn, and multiple black bags sat out front. "Looks like the place is cleaned out." I grabbed a bag. "Let's take these to my place. We can go through them, then cart them to the dumpster."

"We're stooping kind of low here." Still, she hoisted two bags over her shoulders and marched toward my cottage.

By the time Grandma joined us, my floor was covered with papers. We'd started making two piles; one to look at closer and one to toss. When she opened the door, the papers blew together and into every corner of the room.

"Storm is coming. What in the world are the two of

you doing?"

"Going through the bags that came out of Maybelle's cottage. Now, we have to start all over."

"Good thing I'm here to help you." Grandma grinned and knelt beside us. "You go gather up all those ones that blew and I'll tell you what else I found out."

"You can talk while I gather." I kicked off my shoes and crawled under the kitchen table.

"Bob Satchett is missing a watch."

"I know that."

"I bet you didn't know it was a special watch."

I glanced over my shoulder. "Define special."

"Seems it has a thicker back than most watches. He kept his bank information written on a slip of paper and stuffed in the back." She grinned. "I bet Maybelle stole that watch, took out the information, and that's in here somewhere."

Maybe, but my guess is that Dave had already found the bank information. "We'll keep looking, but my bet is that it's been found. We need to get into Heath's cottage."

"That shouldn't be hard," Grandma said. "Just come on to the man. He'll open the door fast enough."

I shook my head. "He'll let me in once I explain why we want in. He wants his name cleared more than anyone."

At least, I hoped. If it turned out Heath was the guilty party, my heart would break.

10

I took a deep breath, left my cohorts at home, and marched down the flagstone to Heath's cottage. I rapped three times and waited, hoping, praying, Dave hadn't returned. If he had, I'd think of some silly reason for the late visit.

Heath answered the door, buttoning a shirt over six pack abs and arms to make a girl swoon. I yanked my thoughts away from his physique. "Is Dave home?"

"No, why?"

"Great." I pushed him inside.

He stumbled back before getting his footing. "What's going on, Shelby? Somehow, I don't think you're here for a make-out session."

I wished. "Dave took something from Maybelle's cottage today, and I think I know what it is. I just need to find it. Come with me to his room." I headed for the guest room.

"We can't snoop through his things without

permission." He limped after me.

"Just keep a watch out. It's a little slip of paper…" Where did I look first? The man hadn't unpacked. Boxes lined the walls. Seriously? This much stuff for maybe a week's work? I headed for the dresser.

Business cards, receipts, and a tiny folded square of paper. Bingo! I slipped it into my pocket. "Heath, I found—"

Dave entered the cottage, a puzzled look on his face. "Hello?"

"Yeah, uh, hello, I'm, uh, here to see Heath. Yeah, that's it." I needed to think of something fast. I grabbed the collar of Heath's shirt and yanked him close, pressing my lips against his. He stumbled, taking us both to the floor. His elbow connected with my ribs, knocking the breath out of me. At least, I think it was the elbow. It might have been the kiss.

"Should I leave again?" Dave's question pulled me to my senses.

"Help me up," I whispered harshly to Heath. When he did, I painted on a smile. "That was fun. We should do it again sometime." I sailed out the door. It wasn't until I got outside that I realized my comment could be completely misunderstood by Dave. No help for it now. I had what I'd come for.

"Hold up." Heath caught me halfway home. "What was that all about?"

"I had to think of something."

He chuckled, wrapping his arms around my waist and pulling me close. "You should hear what Dave is saying. He's making you out to be quite the naughty girl."

"Really?" My gaze landed on his lips.

"Yeah. I have a question." His husky voice sent shivers through me.

"Yes?"

"What is a real kiss from you like, because that one was pretty hot." He cupped my face and kissed me with such tenderness tears sprung to my eyes. The kiss deepened, making my blood boil and my knees weak. "That's how I kiss someone," Heath said with a wink. He turned and sauntered down the sidewalk, whistling.

Back at the cottage, I waved the square of paper, ignored Grandma's and Cheryl's questions, and strolled as if in a trance to my room. I didn't want to share what had happened. Not until I had time to process the kiss.

~

After a sleepless night of reliving the kiss, then deciding it was nothing more than a teasing gesture in response to my clumsy roll on the floor kiss, I crawled out of bed and headed to the kitchen for a glass of green tea. I'd need extra caffeine to function that day.

"Hey, woman who strolled in last night like she was hiding something." Cheryl popped up from the sofa. "What's on the agenda for today?"

"I'm thinking the bushes around Bob and Myrna's cottages need trimming." I poured tea from a pitcher into a glass. I held it up to see if Cheryl wanted some. She shook her head no, so I continued. "Which means skipping breakfast."

"Oh, goody. Snooping. You get started. I'll run to the buffet, grab some things we can eat with our hands and find you."

"Perfect." Other than hanging around those two cottages for a bit, I had no idea where to go from there. The paper I'd taken from Dave's room burned in my pocket. What did I do with it since I didn't have the watch? Sometimes, I didn't think far enough ahead.

The responsible thing to do would be to turn it over to Officer Lawrence. Which I would do as soon as I made a copy. I spread it out on the kitchen table and snapped a picture of it with my phone. Ta da. I was now ready to be responsible the next time I saw the gruff police officer.

I was waylaid by Alice the moment I stepped from my little home. "Is there something you wanted me to do?"

She lifted her chin. "I expect a certain…decorum from my employees."

Ah. Dave snitched. "It isn't what it looked like."

"Rolling on the floor with the handyman isn't what it looks like?"

"No, ma'am."

She made a noise in her throat. "Make sure it isn't. Discretion, Shelby, please." She whirled and marched away like a drunken cow. I really wanted to teach her to walk in heels.

Reputation ruined, but one step closer to finding out who killed Maybelle, I went to the storage shed and grabbed shears and a rake. I might have a mystery to solve, but I was also getting paid to do a job.

Heath stepped out of his cottage, a brace on his leg, and tossed me a wave.

I ducked my head and increased my pace. There was no way I was ready to face him in the light of day.

"Ah, something happened between the two of you last night," Cheryl sang on her way past me toward the dining room.

My face heated, and I kept on my path, not

breathing until I reached Myrna's cottage. Her kitchen curtains were parted a bit and I was able to peek in as I worked.

She glanced up from washing a mug and screamed, then slammed the window open, catching me in the forehead. "What are you doing?"

A lot of people seemed to be asking me that question lately. "Trimming the bushes." I put a hand to my head, relieved there was no blood. I didn't handle blood well.

"There's no need to stare in windows while trimming." She slammed the window shut and closed the curtains.

Great. No clues coming from her. I quickly finished the work there and moved to Bob's cottage where he and Alice argued in the living room. Lucky for me the window was open. I trimmed the bushes just out of direct sight.

"I'm telling you, I'll get my rent caught up next week," Bob said. "My account's been cleaned out. If I catch who did it, I'll kill them."

"One more week, Bob. If I don't have the full amount due, I'll have to evict you." Alice stormed outside and slammed his door.

Bob followed. "Don't threaten me, Missy. My garbage disposal has been broken for a week! I have grounds not to pay."

She shook her head and continued on her way, passing Mr. Weasley.

He approached Bob. "I have a leaky faucet. Ever since the handyman got hurt things are falling apart around here. I thought we had a substitute."

"I haven't seen hide nor hair of the man if we do.

Come on in for coffee."

I'd hoped the invitation would warrant a bit more information, but all they did was complain about the lack of repairs. Yep. I'd have to fire Dave. Better yet, I'd try to get Alice to do it. She was the manager, after all.

I finished at Bob's cottage and headed for the dining room. Since Cheryl had yet to bring me my breakfast, and my stomach was letting me hear about it, I needed to search for my own food.

Most of the buffet had been cleared, but there was a blueberry muffin and one cold sausage patty. I grabbed both and headed for Alice's office.

Her door was partially open so I gave a soft knock and entered. Alice had her head down. She sighed when I entered.

"I guess I should close the door if I want privacy." She glanced up. "Yes, Shelby?"

"I'm sorry to bother you, but there are complaints about the lack of repairs. I want you to fire Dave Mason. Since Heath is no longer using crutches, he can handle small repairs. Dave didn't do anything anyway." I gripped the back of a chair.

"You hired him."

"You're the manager."

"Very well. Find him and send him to me. Anything else?" She straightened and crossed her arms. "The grounds are starting to shape up by the way. Oh, and the greenhouse will be repaired today. The two functions you've headed up have been a great success. You're an asset to our community."

"Thank you." Warmth infused me. I'd rarely gotten compliments at my teaching job. I knew I'd done well because of my reviews, but to have someone call me an asset gave me the warm fuzzies. "I'll try and find Dave."

"See if you can't get those cleaning girls to hurry up with Maybelle's cottage, would you? I have an interested tenant."

I nodded. Just like that, she gave me another of her jobs to do. Was I the gardener or her assistant? I turned to leave and ran into Officer Lawrence, literally. "Sorry."

He shook his head. "Miss Johnson, do you have a minute?"

"Seems everyone wants a minute," Alice said, waving a hand for me to leave.

"Miss Hart, don't go far, please." Officer Lawrence gave me the look that said stay. "I have questions for you, too. Please wait in the lobby."

I did as ordered, sitting on a faux leather loveseat and twiddled my thumbs. Maybe I'd get really lucky and Dave Mason would stroll through the door and I could send him to Alice. No such luck. No one came through the front doors. I didn't know who was more bored; me or the receptionist who filed her nails. A plaque on the desk said her name was Teresa Givens. Did Shady Acres really need a receptionist? It seemed as if Alice could do the job well enough. She was pretty good about putting off her responsibilities on me.

I jumped to my feet when Office Lawrence came my way and pulled the folded piece of paper from my pocket. "I think one of the watches in Maybelle's box that you have belongs to Bob Satchett. This paper, his bank information, should have been inside the watch, but was stolen by Dave Mason, our temporary, soon to be fired, handyman."

When I stopped for breath, he took the paper. "How did you come by this?"

"You don't want to know."

He gripped my elbow and pulled me behind a plastic fichus tree. "I don't know how you came by this information, Miss Hart, but meddling in an active police investigation is dangerous. I must ask you to stop."

"But Birdie asked me to solve her friend's murder."

"There is more going on here than you know. Stop snooping." He released me. "Thank you for the paper, and yes, the watch belongs to Mr. Satchett. We'll be returning the stolen items soon."

I crossed my arms. "You had a question for me?"

"Not really a question." He ran his hand through his hair. "Your friend, the tall gal? She's been hit over the head. She's in your cottage refusing to go to the hospital."

"Define hit over the head."

"Someone hit her on her way back from breakfast." He narrowed his eyes. "This is what happens when two clueless young women meddle where they have no business. Walk with me."

We headed toward the cottage, me walking as fast as my short legs would go.

"Your Grandmother is with her," Officer Lawrence said. "I have one more thing to ask."

"Shoot." I reached for the doorknob of my cottage.

"Do you happen to know where Dave Mason is? No one has seen him since before daylight."

11

"*F*ind him and send him to me, Miss Hart. I'll be around." Officer Lawrence turned and headed out the back door of the main building.

I'd been ordered by two people to find Dave Mason. I had a strong urge to bop him upside the head once I did. First, I wanted to check on Cheryl.

She laid on my sofa and held an ice pack to the back of her head. "I guess you heard," she said, keeping her eyes closed.

"Officer Lawrence told me. Why don't you tell me what happened?" I sat on the coffee table while Grandma handed me a glass of tea.

"I dropped our breakfast." She opened one eye. "I had my hands full and was headed out to find you when I rounded the corner of the building and found myself face down in the petunias."

"Better than face up under the daisies," Grandma cackled.

"I am not in a humorous mood." Cheryl closed her eye again. "When Shelby finds out who hit me, I'm going to clobber them."

"Aren't you still going to help me solve this mystery?" I glanced between the two of them. "I also have a job to do."

"I thought it would be a lark," Cheryl said. "A misunderstanding. I didn't expect to get hurt."

I wisely left out the thought that snooping might very well get us killed. "Fine. You can ramble around here bored for the rest of your vacation." I got to my feet. "There's ibuprofen in the medicine cabinet in the master bath."

"I didn't say I wasn't going to help." She opened an eye again. "I just didn't expect to get whacked."

"Don't be such a big cry baby." I took a sip of my tea, grimaced at the over amount of sugar, and headed for the door. "I'm glad you're okay. I've been ordered to find Dave Mason."

"Be careful," Cheryl called. "Grandma, maybe you should go with her."

"Good idea. We'll lock the door behind us." Grandma grabbed the large sparkly bag she called a purse and followed me. "Don't be cross with her. I gave her a pain pill. They affect her in a weird way. She'll be excited to be singled out by morning."

"I should never have told Birdie I'd look into things. I'm getting nowhere, anyway." I led Grandma to Heath's cottage. We might as well look in the obvious place first.

We knocked and got no answer. Either he and Heath were off working, my guess was only Heath was working, or Dave was wandering the grounds in an attempt not to be found. "Let's walk the perimeter, then check the hiking path. I'd finally finished going through all the papers Alice had given me and studied the map included there. We had a fishing lake on the premises, a bike and hiking trail, you name it, Shady Acres had it, and the residents paid the high price of living there.

"I don't think he wants to be found." Grandma pulled out a few pieces of hard butterscotch candy from her purse and offered me one.

I shook my head. "He's a lazy one, for sure. Heath!" I spotted him limping toward the pool area.

He stopped and waited for us. "What's up?"

"I'm looking for Dave."

"Aren't we all?" He scowled. "I asked him to clean the pool filter. He carried the tools here, but there's no sign of him and the filter is still clogged. What's weird is his hat is here. He never goes anywhere without that ratty thing."

True. I scrunched up my mouth and did my best to figure out where he could have gotten off to. "He was at breakfast, right?"

"No, he was gone when I woke up this morning."

"That's a couple of hours ago," Grandma said. "Someone is bound to have seen him unless there is a part of this community closed off to the residents."

I glanced at Heath. "Is there?"

"A couple of private storage sheds, an old koi pond in need of repair, and the dock which is sagging. All on my to-do list."

"Let's check the dock. Maybe he took the day off to go fishing." I waved Heath ahead of us. "How's the knee?"

"Better. It'll be sore by night, but improving each

day. That's a good thing. There's a lot to do around here. Alice might like to shuffle her work off on others, but she's doing a good job getting this place up to snuff after the last manager."

"Who was the last manager?"

"He retired. The owner offered him a place here, but he wanted Florida. The community was in sad shape and losing residents before Alice was hired."

My opinion of her improved somewhat. Shady Acres was a lovely place. With a combined effort we could make it a showplace...if I could ever focus on my job and not hunt down killers and lazy employees.

As we walked, I spotted plants that needed replanting, mulch that needed replacing, some juniper bushes that would make wonderful topiaries, the list went on. Tomorrow, Cheryl could spend more time recuperating. I was going to focus the entire day on the grounds. "Do I have a gardening budget?"

Heath glanced down at me. "I imagine. You'd have to ask Alice."

"Who mows the expansive lawns?"

"She hired someone to do that and the edging. You're only responsible for flowers and bushes."

And anything else she could think up, but he did relieve a bit of my anxiety. While Shady Acres had thirty cottages strategically placed around the grounds, I felt I could keep up with the work load given the chance.

As we walked, Heath's hand kept bumping mine until I finally realized it was a subtle gesture to make physical contact. I narrowed my eyes and mouthed, "No." After all, the kiss I gave him was to cover up for my being in his apartment snooping through Dave's things, not because I wanted in a relationship. That's the last thing I wanted right then, despite Heath's handsomeness.

He gave a playful pout and shrugged. "There's the dock."

"Dave?" I stepped next to the rickety dock and glanced up and down the rocky, tree-lined shore. Several small rowboats in need of paint jobs bobbed in the water. There was no sign of Dave. "Is there a building or anything he could be hiding in?"

"Nothing. If I hadn't found his hat, I'd think he'd left."

"Is his truck here?" Grandma planted fists on her bony hips. "That's the first thing you should have checked."

I hadn't thought to check. "Heath?"

"His truck is here." He looked at Grandma as if offended that she would challenge his intelligence.

"Then, he's here somewhere." She turned and sauntered back the way we'd come.

"Why do you need to find him so badly?" Heath asked, his hand brushing mine again.

"To fire him and Officer Lawrence wants to talk to him about stealing the paper from Bob's watch."

"I'd hide, too." He chuckled. "We should go on a date sometime."

I stopped. "I just got over a bad breakup. I need some time before even thinking about such things. Don't we see enough of each other at work? We're both here twenty-four seven." At least, I was.

"You need to get away once in a while."

Today was Sunday. My day off. Drat. I'd gotten roped into working. "You're right. I'm supposed to be off work today. Once I find Dave, I'm going to town to visit my mother." That's the only way Alice couldn't infringe on my free time.

"You get Sunday and Monday," he told me. "Don't let Alice rob you of those days."

Even better. Cheryl and I would spend the night with Mom, popcorn, chick flicks, and sparkling Moscato. "Let's hurry up and find this man."

We increased our pace as much as Heath's bum knee would allow and caught up with Grandma. "I thought I was going to have to double back," she said. "No more dawdling. I have things to do."

"Like what?" I grinned.

"I have a date with Ted."

"Who's that? Another resident? You sure get around."

She gave me 'that look'. "It's Officer Lawrence, I'll have you know. I do not date around. I date a lot, but only one man at a time." She tossed her hair back and marched ahead of us.

"Feisty." Heath laughed. "That's how you'll be at her age."

"Please." I rolled my eyes. "She's way more fun than me, and I would not be caught dead in animal print leggings."

"No, just frilly dresses, short shorts, and rain boots in every color of the rainbow."

He noticed what I wore? "A girl likes to look pretty."

"You'd be pretty in a flour sack."

I opened my mouth to speak, then clamped it shut. For once, I was at a loss for words.

"The koi pond is right ahead. See the non-working

fountain of Venus? Getting it working again is a top priority of mine. Maybe you could help by procuring some water plants."

I nodded and rushed to where Grandma waved frantically for us to hurry. "I found him!"

"Where?" I couldn't see anyone.

"There. Peering up at me from the algae." She pointed into the pond.

Eyes wide open, a red film skimming the water around him, was Dave. Someone had slit his throat and dumped him. I pulled out my cell phone and dialed Officer Lawrence. "He's in the koi pond."

"What do you mean he's in the pond? Is he drunk and taking a swim?"

"No, sir. He's dead."

"Stay there. I'll be there in a second." Click.

"The cavalry is on its way." My stomach heaved and I sagged against the goddess Venus. So much…blood. I turned and threw up.

Heath put an arm around my waist and led me to a nearby bench. "Way to hold it together until you phoned the police."

"Yeah, I'm good during the emergency and fall apart afterwards." I bent over and put my head between my knees.

"Here." Grandma thrust a bottle of water at me. "I'm always prepared."

"Thank you." Her bag must weigh a ton. I've never needed anything when with her that she couldn't provide.

"I guess you won't have to fire him now, bless his heart." She unwrapped a piece of candy and handed it to me. "Take it this time. It will help with your sour mouth."

I popped the candy in my mouth and kept my gaze averted from the pond. Not that I could see any part of Dave. No, he was covered with water and slime, and…stop it! I switched my mind to thinking of flowers and butterflies.

"Who do you think would want to kill him?" Grandma moved back to the fountain. Nothing ever seemed to bother her. "Bob, I suppose, but he would be the first suspect so it doesn't make sense. Do you think the same person killed him is the one who killed Maybelle?"

"It's a good assumption. Both of them seemed to have a talent for being where they shouldn't." Of course, Dave was supposed to be cleaning out Maybelle's cottage, but he wasn't supposed to take anything.

"I hope they don't try and pin his death on me, too. After all, I was the last one to see him alive." Heath sat next to me, his shoulders sagging.

"That's a very good assumption, Mr. McLeroy." Office Lawrence marched to our side. "I will definitely have some questions for you."

"See?" Heath sighed.

I actually felt sorry for him. "I don't think Heath would have hit Cheryl, Officer Lawrence. It's quite possible that the person who hit her, killed Dave, don't you think?"

"A good possibility." He pulled a small notepad from his pocket. "Now, Mr. McLeroy, when was the last time you laid eyes on the victim?"

12

After making sure Heath wasn't going to be hauled to the local jail on suspicion of murder, I packed an overnight bag, gathered up Cheryl, and headed to Mom's house. Grandma promised to meet us there later after her date. The most important thing was…I would be away from Shady Acres for a night.

"Girls." Mom greeted us with open arms. "I've movies, popcorn, pizza, you name it."

I gave her a hug. "Sounds like just what I need."

She immediately ushered us inside and ordered Cheryl to spread out on the sofa. "We'll have your head as good as new in no time."

"Impossible," I said, reaching for a slice of mega-meat pizza. "It's been damaged for years."

"Very funny." Cheryl did as ordered, claiming the entire sofa, leaving the two easy chairs to me and Mom. Grandma would have to fend for herself when she arrived.

"Sit." Mom waved her hand. "Tell me all about your job and these deaths. Yes, I know about the second one. Grandma texted me."

"She spreads news faster than a twister." I plopped into a chair and toed off my shoes. "There isn't a lot to tell. I'm no longer a suspect, but the handyman seems to be the primary person of interest. One of the residents has asked that I help find out who killed her friend, but I've come up against dead ends so far."

"Poor choice of words, dear." Mom shook her head. "I'm not sure I like you getting involved."

I shrugged. "Until Cheryl got hit, there hadn't been any danger. I've thought about pulling back."

"No!" Cheryl sat up. "We can't stop now. Whoever hit me thinks we know something. We need to find out what that something is before they come after us again."

"Fine. Let's spend our eating time trying to figure out just what in the world is going on?" I wiped my mouth with a napkin. "Maybelle was killed by rat poison with someone else's teeth in her mouth. Dave Mason had his throat slit after stealing Bob's bank information, then tossed in the algae-filled koi pond." I grabbed another slice of pizza. "Other than Maybelle being a snoop, and Dave a lazy thief, we have no motive."

"Two different methods of death," Mom said. "Are you sure it's the same killer?"

"I don't want to contemplate two killers at Shady Acres." I shuddered. One was one too many.

"You can't discount the possibility."

"Your Mom's right." Cheryl sat up and reached for a slice. "What if?"

"We still need motives." Whether one killer or two, people didn't tend to kill without reason, unless they were a serial killer or something. Holy Cow! Shady Acres didn't have a serial killer, did they? The pizza sat like a congealed lump in my stomach. I reached for a glass of Moscato.

"What if…" Mom put a finger to her lips. "You have an unsavory character living there and Maybelle in her snooping, and Dave in his stealing, came across information best kept hidden."

"Makes sense, I suppose. Dave could have found out whatever Maybelle knew while he was stealing. Funny thing is, Maybelle was a thief, too. Petty things like jewelry, prescription meds, and watches. Mom, I think you hit it on the head." I winked at Cheryl.

"You're a regular standup comedian today," Cheryl said. "Now, we need to figure out just what our thieving little friends saw that they shouldn't have."

"I know the answer to that question." Grandma sailed through the front door and smacked Cheryl's legs until she moved them. "Someone at Shady Acres is not who they say they are."

The rest of us stared at her as if she'd turned blue. "How do you know that?" I asked.

"Lawrence let it slip during a rather heated make-out session."

Eew. Too much information, as usual. "I don't suppose he told you who the person is?"

"No. Once he realized what he'd said, he clammed up and left. That's why I'm here early." She poured herself a glass of wine. "I hope you have another bottle, Sue Ellen. This won't last long with four of us."

"Of course, I do, Mother." Mom sighed and moved

to the kitchen, returning a moment later with an ice bucket and sparkling almond champagne.

"I said wine, not that sissy stuff." Grandma frowned.

"Then you should have brought your own."

"I have some in the car. Now, where were we?"

"An imposter at Shady Acres." I said. "Do we know whether it's a man or a woman? There are thirty cottages and I haven't met everyone yet."

"Then, you'd best get busy, girlie." Grandma grinned. "Meet them all and weed out the least likely suspects."

How in the world was I supposed to do that short of knocking on thirty doors? I'd tried mingling at a social event, but not everyone attended. The koi pond! I could go door-to-door for donations to fix the beautiful structure. I explained my idea.

"I'm sure there's money in the budget, maybe, but this would get the citizens involved and give me a reason to knock on doors. The only problem is, I'll have to use my off time to do it."

"What else are you going to do in your evenings?" Grandma asked. "It isn't as if you have a gentleman friend."

"Thanks for pointing that out." I narrowed my eyes. "Am I not allowed time to grieve over my canceled wedding?"

"Pshaw! That's the best thing that could have happened to you. Marrying that pompous donkey would have made you miserable."

She was right, but it still rankled when she pointed out my single status. "Cheryl, you'll have to go with me when I do this. I'm not doing any investigating alone."

"Agreed." She gulped back her wine and laid back, putting her legs in Grandma's lap. "Look what happened to me. If someone were to hit your skinny little self, you'd break."

I glared at her. "Let's go over the people we do know and see if they should be added to a suspect list. Mom, do you have a notepad we can use?"

"Yep." She moved some magazines from the top of the coffee table and retrieved a notebook with fluorescent flowers. Inside the notebook was a matching ink pen. "I was going to journal, then found it too much trouble."

"Here are the names I'm familiar with. Heath McLeroy—"

"He's too handsome to kill anyone," Grandma argued.

I gave her a look to hush. "Alice Johnson, the manager, Birdie, I still don't know her last name—"

"It's Sorenson," Grandma said, refilling her glass.

"Birdie Sorenson, Harold Ball, the cleaning girls, Amber and Becky, who could easily have found out the same information Maybelle and Dave did. Maybe we should warn them?" When no one answered, I continued. "Myrna Smith, Bob Satchett, Harry Weasley, and Ann Wilson, who I know little to nothing about."

"No one by the name of Weasley ever worked at Cooper Elementary," Cheryl said. "I meant to tell you this morning, but forgot. Head injury, you know? Now, why lie about something like that?"

"He had his reasons, I suspect. I have some names for you." Grandma leaned forward. "Ann Wilson is a former mistress of a US Senator. That might give her motive. Then, there's Leroy Manning. He's a recluse who never comes to any of the meals or socials and only walks the grounds at night. Maybe he's a vampire."

I wasn't sure if she was serious or kidding so I let her comment slide.

"Then, there's Hattie Black, the most rude, sharp-tongued woman you'll ever meet this side of hell."

"Are you listing her because she might be a suspect or because you don't like her?" My pen poised over the paper.

"Both. But I'd give my last bottle of wine that if anyone knows anything about the residents of Shady Acres, it would be her."

"Why?"

"Because I said so? Not buying it? Fine." She huffed. "I caught her sneaking out of Bob's cottage the other night with a grocery bag of items. The man wasn't home at the time."

"Perhaps her reason for being there was legit," Mom said.

"He is the resident Casanova," Cheryl added. "Maybe she carried a change of clothing."

Grandma shrugged one shoulder in an elegant gesture I'd love to master. "Perhaps she did do the walk of shame. Still, I say you keep a close eye on that woman."

"It sounds to me as if that place you work, Shelby, is nothing more than a den of iniquity." Mom glanced at a paint-by-number picture of Jesus on the wall. Her lips moved in a silent prayer. My sweet mother and my fun-loving grandmother were so different it was difficult to know they shared the same DNA.

"It does look that way, Mom, but don't worry, I won't fall into that trap." I closed the notebook. "We have a good list of suspects. It's a beginning anyway."

"You have thirty cottages full of suspects," Grandma said. "Those are only the ones you know."

"Thanks for pointing that out." I could become overwhelmed very quickly. Tears sprang to my eyes as was customary when I was feeling sorry for myself. If I could find a way to get out of this promise to Birdie, I would. I wasn't a detective. All I wanted to do was dig in the dirt and care for my plants.

"What's wrong, sweetie?" Mom gave me a concerned look. "Tummy hurt?"

"I need to learn to say no."

"To three slices of pizza?"

"That and people wanting things I'm not qualified to do." I sighed. "Who am I to think I can solve a murder?"

"A single gal looking for excitement," Grandma said. "If you had a man, you wouldn't have to look at death to spice things up."

I rolled my eyes. "You have a man but that doesn't stop you from snooping."

"I'm an old lady. The rules are different."

"I'm going to bed." I stood and set my glass on the coffee table. "Good night, everyone. Cheryl?"

"Yeah, I'm coming. Not exactly the chick flick kind of night I'd hoped for, but we did get a suspect list going. At least the evening wasn't a total waste of time."

"Let's go to the pancake house for breakfast," Grandma called.

I lifted a hand to let her know I'd heard and headed

to my childhood bedroom on the second floor. Mom really did need to sell this old place. It was too big for her to upkeep on her own.

Cheryl and I climbed into the full size bed we'd slept in so many times as children. "I seem to remember my bed being bigger."

"We've grown since then." Cheryl flipped to her side.

"*You've* grown since then." I've been the same size since seventh grade. The only changes were some boobs and a little roundness in the hips. In the right clothes, I'd look like a twelve-year-old boy.

"Measure yourself on the doorpost in the kitchen. I bet your two inches taller." Cheryl laughed, shaking the bed. "You're a garden gnome now, instead of a sprite."

I slammed my pillow into her gut. Before I could take a breath, she landed hers upside my head, knocking me from the bed. "You always could get the best of me in a pillow fight." I laughed so hard, I couldn't get to my feet. Perhaps the evening was exactly what I needed after all.

"Get up." She held out her hand and pulled me back onto the bed. "Don't despair over this whole murder thing. You'll be rewarded for helping someone receive justice."

"If I don't die."

"If you die, you go to heaven. No biggie."

"I'd like to get married and have children first."

"With someone like Heath?" She elbowed me.

"Perhaps." I giggled into my pillow. Amazing how this pink and purple room reverted us back to our youth in both actions and minds. "He is dreamy."

She roared with laughter. "I haven't heard that

phrase in a long time."

A knock on the wall signaled that Mom was tired of our noise. Instead of quieting us, we laughed harder. I had my mother, my grandmother, and my best friend. What more did I need?

At that moment, I felt as if I could tackle anything the world threw at me.

13

*T*he next morning the four of us girls went to The Pancake House and crowded into a corner booth. We ordered coffee immediately and studied the menu although nothing had changed in the months since I'd been there. Donald hadn't liked the country atmosphere or the simple fare.

"What's first on the agenda when we go back?" Grandma closed her menu.

I decided on Belgian waffles with strawberries. "I'll start going door-to-door on the pretense of asking for donations for the koi pond. I mean, I'll actually ask for the donations, but I'll ask some questions, too. Cheryl, you come with me. Your height might intimidate people into giving money."

"Great. Use the giant to scare old people into giving money." Grandma slapped the table. "Outrage!"

"May I take your order?" A smiling, middle-aged waitress stopped at our table.

"Yes, thank you. I'll take the two eggs, bacon and

hash browns." Grandma patted her stomach. "I may be little, but I have a mighty big appetite."

We all placed our orders, then the moment the waitress left, Grandma attacked me again. "You should be ashamed of yourself."

"Fine. You go with me, then."

"Nah, Cheryl can go. I've got plans." She dug into her purse and pulled out a tube of bright pink lipstick.

I swore she would drive me insane before the month was out. "Do you mind, Cheryl?"

"No. I did come to help, and it'll beat sitting in the cottage all day. Of course, you are still officially off duty today, so let's make some time to soak up sun by the pool."

"Agreed."

"Don't look now but Mr. Handsome just limped in with Officer Lawrence." Cheryl elbowed me.

"Stop doing that. You're going to leave bruises." I glanced toward the door.

"I told you not to look."

"How can I not look when you tell me not to look?" My gaze locked with Heath's troubled one. "You don't think he's about to be arrested, do you?"

"At a pancake house?" Grandma shook her head. "Maybe you aren't as bright as I thought you were."

"Hey. Alright, now." No need to get mean.

The two men were seated at a table too far away for us to hear their conversation, and so close that I was on the edge of my seat, literally, straining to hear. I almost slipped off the slippery vinyl seat. Catching myself before I made a scene, my arm knocked over my glass of water. Liquid ran across the table and into Cheryl's lap.

"Great. It looks like I wet my pants." She dabbed at her lap with a napkin.

Officer Lawrence glared our way, then said something to Heath. They stared at us as if we were little green martians, then resumed their conversation.

"Way to be inconspicuous. Sue Ellen, do something with your daughter." Grandma pulled a mirror from her bag and applied the lipstick.

"She takes after you. There's no help for her." Mom's remark was so deadpan that we were all silent for a second, before bursting into laughter.

I really needed to come home more often. "You're killing me, Grandma."

The waitress brought our breakfast. For a few minutes, the only sound at our table was the clink of silverware against cheap porcelain dishes.

I snuck a peek at Heath's table. He and Lawrence had pie and coffee in front of them. I should have had pie for breakfast. What a great idea. I'd try to remember that next time.

"I taught you better than to stare," Mom said, tapping the back of my hand with her spoon.

"I can't help it. I want to know what they're talking about."

"Find out later."

Shrugging, I turned back to my meal. When we'd finished, Heath and Officer Lawrence were also preparing to leave. I grabbed Heath's arm. "Fill me in later," I whispered.

He nodded and followed the cop out the door. From the look on his face, whatever had transpired between the two of them wasn't good.

Back at Mom's I repacked my overnight bag,

kissed her goodbye, and invited her to come to dinner one night that week. With Cheryl and Grandma flanking me, we headed to my pretty little Mustang, then back to Shady Acres.

"I hope knocking on thirty doors accomplishes something," I said, emptying my bag into the laundry basket. "If not, it will be an awful waste of time."

"Whatever money you lack for the pond, ask your grandmother. You told me your grandfather left her well off. She can use it as a tax deduction," Cheryl said on the way to her room. "Hurry up and let's get going."

I eyed a pair of rain boots in the corner, then decided against wearing them. I wasn't on the clock that day. What I did was on my own time. "I'm ready." I'd brought the colorful suspect notebook home with me from Mom's and, tucking it under my arm, waited outside the cottage for Cheryl.

Heath came down the walkway at a fast clip, grabbed my arm, and pulled me behind a bush. "I don't have much time. Officer Lawrence is talking to Alice."

"What's happening?" I searched his face.

"They found my other glove in the pond with Dave."

"That doesn't make sense. Why would one glove be by Maybelle and one by Dave? Only an idiot would make that mistake twice."

"It still doesn't look good for me."

"Are they arresting you?"

He shrugged. "Lawrence hinted at such. It all depends on Alice's endorsement."

I stepped back. "Why?"

"Didn't you know? She's Lawrence's niece. They're close. If she'll vouch for me, then he's agreed to not lock me up on her say so."

What kind of police force did this town have? "I've never heard of such a thing."

"I have to go." He gave me a quick kiss on the cheek. "Keep trying to clear my name, okay? I'll catch up with you at lunch, if I'm still a free man." He whirled and jog-limped back to the main building.

When I stepped around the corner, Cheryl was waiting, arms crossed, a scowl on her face. "I was about to give up on you."

I told her what Heath had said. "Isn't that strange? I didn't know cops worked that way."

"They work however they want. Let's start knocking. Maybe we'll find out something to help your boyfriend."

My face heated, remembering the sweet kiss on the cheek and the steamier one from a couple of nights ago. "He isn't my boyfriend."

"Then why is your face all red?" She giggled. "Let's start at cottage number one and work that way so we don't lose our place."

"Spoken like a teacher."

I approached cottage number one which looked as if it had recently received a new coat of paint and knocked. Good for Heath. Thinking about him made me want to run to the main building and see whether he'd been carted away in handcuffs. Why was someone framing him? It's obvious that's what was happening. No one would kill an old woman, drop a glove, then drop the partner to the glove next to a different dead body. It didn't make any sense.

"Yeah." A woman with coal black hair and piercing gray eyes opened the door.

"Good morning. I'm Shelby—"

"I know who you are." She crossed her arms over a bony chest. "What do you want?"

I blinked rapidly, then gained my composure. "We're taking donations for repairs to the koi pond and was wondering—"

"I pay enough rent to cover those kinds of things." She slammed the door in our faces.

"Well, I have no idea who that rude woman was, nor did we gain any information."

"We need a master list of who lives where," Cheryl said. "Do you think the receptionist will give us one?"

"It's worth a try." Maybe I could get a peek as to whether Heath was still around.

We hurried to the main building where the receptionist had changed up her daily chore. Instead of filing her nails, she painted them a turquoise blue. I cleared my throat twice before she glanced up.

"Sorry," she said. "But, I didn't want to mess up." She blew on her nails. "What do you need?"

"A list of which residents live in which cottages." I leaned on the counter.

"Well, I guess that's okay, since you work here and all. My nails are wet. The list is on the computer under resident list. It also has their phone numbers." She rolled her chair back to give me access.

"Have you seen the handyman, Heath, lately?" I asked, searching her computer documents.

"Yeah, some old cop took him out of here."

My heart dropped to my knees and tears stung my eyes. "In handcuffs?"

"No. They headed to the dining room."

Relief flooded through me in such a wave my

knees almost buckled. I quickly found the file, printed two copies, and almost ran to the dining room with Cheryl right behind me. I'd forgotten to tell Teresa thank you. I'd do it later.

In the dining room, Heath sat alone at a table. At another, Officer Lawrence sat with Grandma. I made a beeline for Heath.

"You're here." I gave him an impulsive hug.

He grinned. "If that's the reception I'll get, I'll try to almost get arrested more often."

"Stop." I sat in the chair next to him, Cheryl taking the other side. "I guess Alice vouched for you?"

"Yeah." His brow furrowed. "Vouched for me quite heatedly. It was embarrassing. I think she has a crush on me."

"Oh." A niggle of jealousy pricked me. "You had no idea?"

He shook his head. "We usually get into an argument because she has an unreasonable demand."

That sounded familiar. "Well, the main thing is you aren't going to jail."

"At least not today. I'm still the primary suspect."

"We're trying to clear your name." I explained how we would be going door-to-door. "We only got as far as cottage one when we realized we had no idea who she was."

"That's Hattie Black. She isn't very nice."

"We figured that out real quick."

He laughed. "What did you say to her?"

"That we're collecting to repair the koi pond." I held up a hand at his protest. "It's all I could think of."

"Alice will have a fit. You need to come up with a better plan. If she finds out, she'll think you're criticizing her job."

"Seriously?" I was determined to ask her as soon as lunch was finished. If we could get donations, she could use the budget elsewhere. With all the small things that needed doing, and the weekly social functions she wanted me to plan, money saved was a good thing.

I spotted her entering the room and excused myself to catch her before someone caught her in a conversation. "Alice."

"Shelby." She tilted her head.

"I was wondering whether you would have a problem if I asked the residents for donations to repair the koi pond."

"Why?" Her eyes narrowed. "Heath is working on that."

"I know, but, I thought if the residents had a hand in its restoration, they might feel a sense of pride. We could have an unveiling party."

She wrinkled her nose in thought. "As long as no one thinks it's because we're short on funds. We aren't. It's just that repairs take time and if anything, we're short staffed. Corporation won't let me hire anyone else."

"I'm sure no one will think that. Remember…a penny saved is a penny earned, my grandfather always said." I grinned and turned.

"Oh, and, Shelby?"

"Yes, ma'am?" I glanced over my shoulder.

"Hurry and clear Heath's name, please. I can't move forward in a relationship with him as long as he's a murder suspect."

14

*R*ather than begin my day going door-to-door, I decided to speak with some of the residents at breakfast the next morning. It would save time and foot pain. Since Alice gave her approval, I could approach others with a bit more confidence than the day before.

I grabbed a pastry from the buffet and sat at the table with Harry Weasley and Hattie Black. Neither spoke to each other. Instead, they leaned over their plates like they were starving. Neither looked up when I sat down, either. “Excuse me.”

Harry peered through thick glasses. “Yeah?”

“Good morning. I’ve already spoken to Ms. Black, but we’re asking the residents of our lovely community to donate funds toward restoring the koi pond. It’ll be tax deductible and allow renovating funds to be delegated elsewhere. May we count on your support?”

“Yeah, sure.” Harry pulled out his wallet and tossed me a fifty dollar bill. “Hattie, pay the girl.”

Hattie rolled her eyes and handed me a twenty from inside her bra. "Don't bother me about money again. I'm not as generous as Weasley, here."

I took her money with my fingertips. "Thank you both, very much." I slid the cash into an envelope in the back of my notebook. "Did either of you know the victims very well?"

"Victims of what?" Hattie peered at me over her glasses. "Oh, the dead people. No, not more than anyone else here. I don't usually come to the meals, but I'm short on groceries. This…" she pointed at me, "is why I stay to myself. People always want something."

Harry straightened and crossed his arms. "Why are you asking about them?"

"It's sad and a little scary, don't you think? To have two residents murdered?"

"Most people get what they got coming." He picked up his empty plate and deposited it on a sideboard before leaving the room.

As if noticing she was alone with me, Hattie leaped to her feet and did the same.

I almost wanted to smell myself to see if I stunk. Instead, I sighed and moved to the next table where Myrna and Bob were sitting.

"You look like you're drumming for money," Bob said with a scowl.

I gave him my pitch, not expecting much in return. My eyes widened when he wrote me a check for a hundred dollars. "Why, thank you."

"That old pond is an eyesore, especially now that there's been a body in there. People need something new to look at. Pay up, Myrna."

"I'm on a fixed income."

"From your dead husband." He motioned his head toward me. "Everyone knows you don't need to worry about money for the rest of your life."

"Fine." She also wrote a check for a hundred dollars.

I leaned my elbows on the table and lowered my voice. "Are you two worried about the murders? It's as if we aren't safe leaving our cottages after dark."

"Who says Maybelle was murdered at night?" Myrna shook her head. "No, I saw her early the morning she died. So did you, if memory serves me right. She was looking for her teeth, as usual. Now, that fat handyman…well, I saw him wandering around after dark. Looked mighty suspicious to me."

"Did you see anyone else out and about?"

She glanced at the ceiling and thought for a moment. "One of the cleaning girls was coming home. Then, of course you've got the vampire, Leroy Manning. He's not really a vampire. We just call him that because he only comes out at night. Oh, and Alice was snooping around. That's all I can think of."

None of who seemed like a killer, except maybe for the vampire. "Thank you both for your donations."

I was heading for another table when Harold Belcher, uh Ball, stopped me. "Heard you're looking for money," he said. "Here's twenty bucks." He shoved it into my hand. "We can't have our staff going without."

"Oh, it's to renovate the koi pond and fountain, Mr. Ball. Not for me, personally." How sweet of him.

"Well, that's a good cause, too." He stepped closer. "Tell your grandmother that I'm a bit perturbed she's shoved me off for that cop. That's no way to treat a man."

My heart skipped a beat. "Did you date Maybelle once?"

His eyes narrowed. "What if I did?"

"Nothing." I forced a smile and walked away as fast as I could. I would have to warn Grandma. What if Harold killed Maybelle because he thought she was cheating on him? It happened in movies and books all the time. Everyone knew that fiction was based on fact, right?

"Cheryl." I approached her at the buffet. "Have you seen Grandma?"

"Not since earlier. She was helping me approach people about donations. She was catching them before they came into the building." She glanced around the room. "It's strange for her not to be here."

"I'm heading to her cottage." My heart settled down around my knees. I would never forgive myself for getting her involved if something bad had happened. "Will you come with me?"

"Of course." Cheryl grabbed a banana and rushed outside with me.

We ran for Grandma's cottage. Finding the door locked, I sent Cheryl for Heath and his master key. While I waited, I circled the cottage looking for a way in. The bathroom window beckoned. Opened about six inches, it would suffice if I could get it pushed up another two or three inches. I found a bucket to stand on and hoisted myself up.

After a few seconds of pushing, the window slid open more. Hooking my arms over the windowsill, I spidermanned my way up the wall. My boots slipped a couple of times, despite their rubber soles, and I found myself hanging half in half out. Nice. I was stuck.

I kept kicking against the outer wall until I slid through, landing in a heap on the bathroom floor. "Grandma?" I squeaked out once I caught my breath. I pushed to my feet and hurried to her bedroom.

By the time Heath and Cheryl arrived and unlocked the front door it was obvious Grandma wasn't home. I sagged onto the sofa, tears welling in my eyes. Mom was going to kill me if I didn't find her. "Where could she be?"

"Maybe we should call Officer Lawrence?" Cheryl suggested.

"Sure." Heath knelt in front of me. "Before we worry, we should see whether she went off with him."

I wiped the back of my hand across my eyes. "I should have thought of that. Will you call?"

He made a face, but dug his cell phone from his pocket. "He's the last person I want to talk to, but I'll do it for you." He punched in the officer's number. "Sir, this is Heath McLeroy. Is Miss Ida with you? No, sir, we haven't seen her in over an hour. Shelby is worried with all that's been going on. See you then." He slid the phone back into his pocket. "She isn't with him."

"What now?" I lunged to my feet. "We have to look everywhere."

Heath grabbed my arm and stopped me from rushing outside. "We can't go off helter-skelter. We need a plan. First, we call Alice and have her make an announcement."

"We can do that?"

He nodded. "Then, either Ida will hear and feel bad for scaring you or maybe one of the residents will come forth and say where they saw her last."

"Okay." I was willing to let him take charge. My brain refused to focus on anything other than the fact Grandma was missing. I plopped back to the sofa.

Cheryl sat next to me, putting an arm around my shoulders. "We'll find her. She's most likely flirting with someone or visiting the salon."

"We have a salon?" I glanced up.

"I thought you read your papers."

"I skimmed them. Did you see how big the stack was?"

"Attention residents. Would anyone who has seen Ida Grayson please contact her granddaughter, our very own Shelby? It seems the woman is missing." Alice's announcement rang out loud and clear.

A knock at the door had me springing to my feet. I darted over and yanked it open only to find Officer Lawrence and not Grandma. "She's still missing."

"I heard the announcement." Instead of his uniform, he wore khaki pants and a deep green shirt. "Where have you looked?"

"Just here."

"Okay, we'll split up. I'll take Cheryl. Heath, you go with Shelby." He handed me a walkie talkie. "Notify the others the moment you see or hear anything."

His matter of fact way of approaching the situation helped put me a bit at ease. "Heath and I will take the area around the greenhouse, then work our way to the lake."

He nodded. "We'll start at the main building. There are a lot of places a person could be. Don't worry. We'll find her." He clapped me on the shoulder.

"Come on, sweetheart." Heath took my hand in his

large, work-roughened one, leaving the other two to head one direction while we headed the other.

"What if she's in the koi pond or under a bench in the greenhouse or floating in the lake? Oh! What if she took a hike and turned her ankle and she's in the woods being stalked by a bear?" Each thought seemed worse than the one before. "Did anyone check the pool?"

"We'll check the pool right now. Stop jumping to conclusions. Chances are greater that she's just fine."

I breathed in then out and in and out until my breathing regulated. If Grandma could see how I was freaking out, she'd pinch me. Get it together, Shelby! Put on your Hart pants and do what needs to be done.

Grandma wasn't at the pool or my cottage. Neither was she in the greenhouse or the koi pond, thank goodness. I spotted the shed where I kept my tools. The lock was busted from the door.

"Heath. Look." I pointed and grabbed a shovel I'd left leaning against the greenhouse.

"Give me that and stay behind me." He took my makeshift weapon.

With me holding on to his belt, we snuck up on the shed. Heath held a finger to his lips and pulled the door open. Sunlight squeezed through the dirty window above the door.

Sitting on a crate, her hands and feet tied, a pillowcase over her head, sat my grandmother. She squealed, the sound garbled.

I quickly removed the pillow case and the gag. "What happened?"

She blinked against the sunlight. "I was taking donations. Someone cried for help. I went around the pool house. The next thing I knew someone put this bag over my head, tossed me over their shoulder and carted me here. I'd say our killer is a man."

My gaze was glued to the note pinned to her blouse.

"Stop snooping or fall the way Maybelle did."

15

*W*hile Heath cut the zip ties keeping Grandma bound to the chair, I pressed the button on the walkie talkie. "Officer Lawrence, she's tied up in the tool shed. We've got her. She's unharmed."

"Don't touch anything. Out."

I hung the walkie talkie on the band of my jeans. "He's on his way."

"This ought to let me off the hook." Heath made the last slash of his knife, freeing Grandma. "I was in plain sight in the dining room when Ida was taken."

Grandma hugged him and planted a kiss on his cheek. "Teddy doesn't think you killed anyone. He just doesn't have anyone else to harass. We need to help him solve this case so he has time to focus on me. Now, get me out of this dark, dirty place. We can wait in the sunshine just as well as in here."

We stepped outside. Heath found an old lawn chair in the shed and dragged it out for Grandma while we leaned against the shed.

"I was so worried." The infernal tears started again as I leaned down and hugged her.

"Dry the tears, sweetie. It'll take more than a kidnapping to do me in." Grandma patted my back. "We must be getting too close to solving this thing."

"I guess." I straightened. "I sure wish I knew what it was we supposedly know." Then, the killer could be behind bars and the danger to the residents of Shady Acres a thing of the past.

"You okay, Ida?" Officer Lawrence rushed toward her and gathered her in his arms.

"Right as rain." Grandma laid her head on his shoulder.

I couldn't help but notice how frail she looked in his arms. Almost like a child and a father. For the first time, I realized this strong woman wasn't immortal and there would come a day when I no longer had her around. The tears welled again. I suddenly wanted my mother. I sent her a text asking her to come for lunch.

Seconds later, she responded with a yes. My day brightened.

"The three of you stay out here." Officer Lawrence placed Grandma on her feet and entered the shed. He stood in the doorway and shined a flashlight around the small interior. "Shelby, come here."

I joined him. "What?"

"See anything amiss?"

"Nothing other than the crate my grandmother was tied up on." It would be hard to tell. I hadn't had time in my myriad of duties to organize the shed.

He made a noncommittal noise and stepped outside. "I'll have the crime scene unit come, but I doubt we'll find anything." With his fingertips, he picked up the note Grandma had ripped from her blouse and dropped. He frowned and carefully placed it on the crate to be submitted as evidence.

Alice tapped her way toward us. "Please, tell me she isn't dead. We can't afford another death."

"I'm glad to see how important I am to you." Grandma drew Alice's attention to her. "As you can see, I'm alive and well." She linked her arm with mine. "Let's go to your cottage. I need a drink."

Alice was speared with four glares from myself, Grandma, Heath, and Cheryl. My bestfriend actually paused in leaving and stared down at the selfish manager before following us. I ducked my head to hide a grin.

"Shelby." Alice called me back. "You, too, Heath."

"I'll meet up with y'all." I turned. "Yes?"

"Now that your grandmother has been found safely, I believe you have work to do, do you not? Heath, too. We have a community to run. There are repairs to be made, grounds to upkeep. I want this to be a showplace. That won't happen if you spend your time doing things that aren't your job."

I had to bite my tongue to keep from telling her that she was always having me do things that were not in my job description. Instead, I nodded and headed for the greenhouse. I had some seedlings to plant and needed to weed the herb garden for starters. That should keep me busy until lunch. Still, I wanted to be in my cozy little home keeping an eye on my precious grandmother.

"I'll be working in the main building fixing the plumbing in the men's restroom if you need me," Heath said, stepping into the greenhouse. "Keep your cell phone handy. I don't like you being alone."

"You're in as much danger as I am."

"Don't worry about me." He tweaked my nose before leaving.

I turned to my seedlings, grinning and blushing like a high school girl with a crush. How could I even think of romance after Donald, and with a murderer on the loose? Not to mention how close Grandma had come to being not only a kidnapped victim, but a dead one. I needed to step up my investigation. It didn't appear as if "Teddy" was any better at catching a killer than I might be.

I placed the seedlings on a tray and carried them to a wheelbarrow. They were destined for the herb garden. I moved back inside the greenhouse in search of the gardening gloves I'd left there. Not finding them, I went to the shed. I could have sworn I'd laid them on the bench in the greenhouse. I frowned. My favorite pair. Pink with red ladybugs. Where could I have put them?

Not finding them either place, I hefted the wheelbarrow with unprotected hands and hoped I wouldn't get a splinter, or worse, callouses. Instead of heading straight for the garden, I made a detour to my cottage to fetch another pair of gloves. I had several, and the lost pair were sure to turn up eventually.

I didn't find Grandma or Cheryl in the cottage. No worries. I fetched my metal pail of gloves from the top shelf of my closet and set them in the wheelbarrow next to the plants. I chose a bright yellow pair with blue ducks and happily headed toward the garden by way of the pool. My happiness drained away like a pulled plug in a bathtub.

Mom laughed and chatted with Grandma and Cheryl, all three with their feet in the hot tub and some kind of tropical drink in their hands. Before lunch! Oh, it looked like fun, and here I was slaving away at my job. I sighed and continued on my way. I had told Cheryl I would have to work. It shouldn't be a surprise to either one of us when I actually did work.

Before long, I was kneeling on a cushioned vinyl pad inserting delicate herb plants into the rich soil and forgetting how much I thought I wanted to swim and hang out rather than nurture little green sprouts of life. From a nearby maple tree, a mockingbird serenaded me. The sun kissed my arms and the back of my neck. The day was beautiful and my family was safe. What did I have to complain about?

If I wanted to, I could focus on the fact that Alice had her arm linked with Heath's as the two of them strolled in the direction of the koi pond. Which reminded me I hadn't finished getting donations. Why did the two of them look so lovey dovey? I narrowed my eyes. I got the impression that Heath didn't particularly like the woman.

Alice's giggle reached me, making my blood boil. She glanced my way and tossed me a wave, no doubt hoping I'd clear Heath's name so she could marry him! I was being ridiculous and I knew it. There was nothing between me and the handyman but some harmless flirtation and what might be a nice friendship. It's best I leave things be.

I kicked at a rock in the dirt, then bent to remove it from my garden. The problem with tossing it aside was the fact it wasn't a rock. I held a clump of polished quartz in my hand. The type tourists buy at roadside tourist traps. I grabbed a trowel from the wheelbarrow and dug a little deeper.

Soon, I had quite a little pile of treasures. A locket with a couple from the early 1900s, a vintage mirror, a pocket watch, and silver comb drastically in need of polishing. Were these more items taken by Maybelle or had they been here before Shady Acres was built, waiting for someone to discover them?

I gathered the items and put them in the wheelbarrow. If Officer Lawrence had a list of stolen items, these things might be on there. If not, I'd clean them up and offer them as prizes for a future Bingo game.

A glance at my watch told me it was time for lunch. I rolled the wheelbarrow back to the toolshed and locked the door with the treasures inside. Once I felt they were secure, I hurried to the main building to wash up in the ladies room for lunch. Hopefully, I could solicit more donations and gain some information.

In the restroom, I washed my hands and arms, then splashed my face with cool water. When I felt presentable again, I rushed to the dining room and filled a plate with a salad and sautéed shrimp. I took a seat at my usual table next to Heath, relieved that Alice was nowhere to be seen.

"Productive morning?" I stabbed a cherry tomato rough enough with my fork that the tines slid off and the tomato sailed off my plate and onto the floor.

"Not really." He shook his head. "I had an unwelcome shadow all morning. Alice seemed to think today was the day she needed to personally show me my duties."

I cheered up immediately. "Of course, you must be polite."

"How was your morning?"

I told him about the items I found in the garden. "Who tilled the dirt?"

"I did, but I never noticed anything." He sat back in his chair. "I'm pretty sure I would have noticed if all those things were lying there."

"They were covered by some dirt. I found them while planting herbs."

"Do you mind letting me see them before you turn them over to the authorities? Maybe I'll recognize one of the items." He glanced around the room. "They sound like they came from the time period when most of these people were young. Since I've been here a little over a year—" he shrugged.

"True. Find me after lunch and I'll take you to the shed."

"That sounds like fun." He winked.

"Stop." I smacked his arm. "You're spoken for." With a grin, I got to my feet and started my trip around the room asking for money. My first stop was the table where my family and best friend sat. "Hey." I plopped next to Mom and gave her a hug. "I suppose Grandma told you what happened this morning."

"Yes, and thank you for finding her." Mom returned my hug. "Is that why you invited me to lunch?"

"You three are all I have," I said, glancing at each of them. "I wanted my family around me, even if for only a few minutes."

"This is all warm and fuzzy," Grandma said, "but there's something I want to tell you that I didn't tell

Teddy."

I leaned forward, almost knocking over Mom's glass of tea in my eagerness. "Really? Is it about your abductor?"

"Yep." She lifted a mug of coffee and gave a sly smile. "I have something to tell you that is common knowledge…Maybelle's memorial service is tomorrow. The secret information is…the man who abducted me wore Polo cologne."

16

*M*aybelle's funeral was held in the garden. Alice had Heath string baby's breath and flowers on the gazebo, making the area around the coffin look more like a macabre wedding than a memorial.

Birdie, as close to family as Maybelle had, sat alone on the front row of white folding chairs. I stood at the end of the aisle and, instead of having people sign a guestbook, I handed out memorial cards with the picture of a rose on the front and the twenty-third Psalm inside. As well-wishers traipsed past me, I couldn't help but sniff the air for a whiff of Polo cologne. What would I do if I smelled it?

I'd heard that killers often attended the funeral of their victim. Officer Lawrence must have heard the same thing because he escorted Grandma to a seat then took a stance off to the side.

"Smell anything?" Cheryl stood next to me.

"No." I secretly hoped I wouldn't. I couldn't abide

Polo cologne. "If I do, I'll alert the dear Teddy Lawrence and let him handle things."

My attention was diverted to the front where Maybelle's polished mahogany casket rested. Alice clapped her hands to get everyone's attention. "There will be food served in the dining room directly after the service."

Of course, there would. It would be lunch time.

A man I'd never met rolled a wooden podium in front of the casket and began a generic eulogy that almost left me in tears. I hadn't known Maybelle, but everyone deserved something personal when folks gathered to say goodbye.

"I feel like I should say something."

Cheryl tilted her head. "Say what?"

I shrugged. "I have no idea. I'd only met her that once and got more of a view of her backend then her face." The dilemma was solved as Birdie took the stand when the officiate sat down.

"Ladies and Gentlemen," Birdie began. "Maybelle was my friend. She might have been a kook—"

Cheryl snorted next to me, then clapped a hand over her mouth. "Sorry."

"—but she didn't deserve to die with someone else's teeth in her mouth." She set a jar containing false teeth on the podium. "Here are Maybelle's teeth, may she rest in peace." Birdie put a hand on each side of the podium as if she were gearing up for a fire and brimstone Sunday sermon. She narrowed her eyes and paused long enough to study the crowd.

"One of you…" she growled the word and pointed with a gnarled forefinger, "killed Maybelle. When I find out who did, you will rue the day. Rue the day, I say!" She pounded the podium, gave a definitive nod, then returned to her seat.

Those in attendance sat silent for a moment, then rose as one and formed a line to parade past the casket. Several glanced at Birdie as they did so, as if expecting her to pounce on them.

"Are you going up to pay your respects?" Cheryl asked.

"I'm not sure. I'd rather watch how the others act and see if I can spot our killer. Why don't you go up and view them from there?"

She shuddered. "Dead bodies scare me. You go up and I'll stay here."

"Fine." I handed her the cards. "We'll compare notes at lunch."

I headed to the front of the line, keeping my gaze averted from the casket. I wasn't afraid of dead people, they couldn't hurt you, but I wasn't a fan of a lifeless wax figure that didn't resemble the person it had once been.

Most of those who filed past Maybelle had impassive faces, but a few stared with a look that told me they hadn't cared much for the woman. These were the people I had the most interest in. I stepped closer to the casket as Bob Satchett stepped forward.

"Keep the watch, you old bat." He dropped a watch with a well-used leather band into the casket.

As he moved past me, I detected the not-so-subtle fragrance of Polo cologne. He wasn't the only one who smelled or left gifts. Harry Weasly dropped a box of denture cleaner in and definitely wore Polo, as did two other men. One dropped in an empty pill bottle, the other a dried flower. Yep, the deceased was not a popular woman.

When the line dwindled and people headed for the dining room, Alice motioned her head in my direction and mouthed something I couldn't understand. I frowned and she repeated the gesture to no avail.

"Go supervise the dining room!" She shook her head and marched to Heath's side. She pulled his head down to whisper something in his ear.

He glanced at me and smiled. Over Alice's shoulder, he pointed to the dining room then motioned that he would join me soon.

I nodded and left to do more of Alice's job. Since when did someone need to supervise the dining room? It wasn't a school cafeteria full of unruly students.

"Get any leads?"

I jumped when Officer Lawrence approached me from behind.

"Four men who wear Polo cologne."

"And, that means…"

Ooops. I forgot Grandma said that was a secret. Too late now. "My grandmother told me last night that the man who abducted her wore Polo."

He sighed heavily. "I've resigned myself to the fact that you ladies are going to snoop. In fact, you're right that the residents may talk to you better than to me. But, I do ask…no, I'm telling you, that I expect to be told anything you find out. This could be a break in the case and not telling me is withholding information. I'll go speak to Ida."

I wanted to wish him luck, but after being reprimanded and left to feel like a child, I decided not to. Instead, I joined Cheryl at our usual table. "Four residents at the service wore Polo cologne. Two of them are men I haven't met." I pointed them out to her.

"Leave that to me." She tugged the neckline of her blouse down a bit to show just enough cleavage to make a man around the age of eighty realize he wasn't dead yet and sashayed over to where the two men were in line to fill their plates.

When she got close, she pretended to trip, causing both men to reach forward and catch her. She faked a limp as they escorted her to a table. Soon, they were both plying her with food and drink and sitting on each side of her.

How did she do that? Maybe I needed to learn the art of flirtation. Were there books written on the subject?

"Next time Alice comes up to me, save me." Heath's breath tickled the hairs on the back of my neck. "This time, she wanted me to remove the items from Maybelle's casket because it was too gross for her to handle. I told her to leave the items. As ill intended as they were, they were gifts."

It was none of my business what she wanted, but it made me feel better for him to tell me. I smiled and told him of the cologne discovery and Cheryl's brilliant plan to find out information from the two men I didn't know.

"I could have told you. The big guy is Marvin Hall. He's an ex-con. Did time for assault. The tall skinny man is William Jamison. He's a retired pharmacist. I've never had a problem with either one of them."

Hmm. Well, they did wear Polo and that made them suspects in my book.

"Do you want something to eat? You got me a plate often enough."

I nodded. "Thank you. Something light." Funerals

always affected my appetite. When my father passed away, there'd been enough food to feed an army, beers passed around in his honor, and jokes to make people cry with laughter. I'd never really understood the partying that went on when someone died. Mom said it was a celebration of the person's life. All I knew was that I missed my father and poor Maybelle had no one except Birdie. Not a lot of reason to party.

Heath brought me a turkey sandwich and fruit at the same time Cheryl collapsed with laughter into the chair next to me. "Oh, those two men are the sweetest things. One of them has been to prison for beating up a man who was hitting his wife, and the other said he could get me free narcotics any time I wanted them. I don't think either one of them killed Maybelle," she said. "But, they definitely didn't like her."

"Explain." I bit into a strawberry.

"Well," she propped her legs on the chair next to her and crossed her ankles. "Marvin said she spread rumors that he was the one hitting his wife, and William, or Billy as he told me to call him, said she threatened to spill the beans about his giving away prescriptions if he didn't write her one for painkillers. Dear Maybelle was not only a thief, but a drug addict."

"Just because Marvin says he wasn't the one beating the woman doesn't mean he wasn't."

"True, but he was very much a gentleman to me." She grabbed a piece of melon off my plate.

"If Miss Ida's abductor wore Polo," Heath added, "then Bob, Harry, Marvin, and William are the primary suspects. We need to find a way to make one of them trip themselves up. What made the killer target Maybelle?"

That was the million dollar question, wasn't it? I had no idea. I glanced at Heath, a wheat-colored curl falling forward over his forehead, then across the room to where Grandma giggled at something Officer Lawrence said. These two people were the reason I wanted to catch Maybelle's killer. Sure, Birdie had asked, and I'd half-heartedly agreed to help her. But, clearing Heath's name and catching the person who took Grandma were top priority. Heath's name was cleared on Alice's say-so, but Grandma's abductor was in this room, more than likely, unless he was Shady Acres's very own vampire, and I intended to make sure he was locked up for a long time.

"I'm going to my cottage." Alice had given the staff the day off, except for the kitchen crew, and I planned on spending some time relaxing. I stood. "I'll hide the key in the gnome," I told Cheryl. "I hope to take a nap."

"All right. I won't be long. A nap sounds like a wonderful idea."

At home, I stashed the key where I'd said, dismissing the idea that it was a common place to hide such a thing and any killer worth his or her salt would know that, and went inside. I kicked off my shoes and removed my earrings, more than ready to put on a pair of baggy shorts and an over-sized tee shirt.

I dropped one of the earrings. Of course it couldn't just fall, it had to roll under the sofa. On my knees, I stretched my arm to reach for it and came in contact with not only the earring, but a piece of paper. I withdrew both and stared at a list of men's names. The very names I had on my own suspect list. Only, this list wasn't in my handwriting.

Had it come from Maybelle's garbage? Why these four men? Was I that close to finding her killer?

I sat back on my knees, certain I was holding the killer's name in my hand. Under their names were a set of numbers that looked suspiciously like a lock combination. Where in Shady Acres would a person need a lock with a combination?

17

"*W*hat are you doing on the floor?" Grandma entered and held the door open for Heath and Cheryl.

I held up my hand for someone to help me to my feet. "I found this under the sofa. It must have fallen there when we were going through Maybelle's garbage." My legs tingled as the blood flow was restored. "Is there any place at Shady Acres where a combination lock is needed?"

"Maybelle's things are stored in a storage room off the main building," Heath said, helping me onto the sofa. "We could look through her boxes."

"Let me change." I dashed to my room and donned the comfy clothes I had intended to put on anyway. No sense in dressing nice to rummage through dusty old boxes.

When I rejoined the others I could tell from Grandma's face that she didn't think the same way in regards to my attire. I ignored her unspoken condemnation, retrieved the key from Cheryl, and moved outside. Hopefully, we could do some snooping without getting caught. I didn't have a good explanation for why we'd be going through a dead woman's things on the day of her funeral.

"While the three of you do that," Grandma said. "I'll keep Teddy busy. I'm only supposed to be gone long enough to check on you."

"Thanks." I kissed her powdered cheek. "I'll tell you what we find at supper."

"Darn toot'n." She grinned, wiggled her fingers in a wave, and sauntered back in the direction of the main building.

I watched until she entered the double doors, not wanting her to go anywhere alone again. "Let's do this." I met Heath's amused glance. "What?"

"You're adorable in those clothes."

Heat traveled from my toes upward and settled in my cheeks. I glared at Cheryl, who snorted behind her hand.

"She looks like a little kid," she said. "There's even a hole in the back of those shorts letting everyone know that she's wearing purple panties."

"Ugh." I raced back inside and changed the shorts to denim capris. So much for comfort. I'd keep the holey shorts for bedtime. Back outside, I lifted my chin. "Now, can we go?"

"Sure thing." Heath jangled a ring of keys. "Follow me."

On the edge of the grounds stood a cement block building almost completely covered by bushes. I really needed to investigate every inch of Shady Acres. I'd had no idea this building was even here.

"This is a long way for you to go when you need to retrieve something." I tried to peer through a crack in the boarded up window.

"I'm trying to get Alice to purchase me a Gator. Then, I'd get more done in less time." He unlocked the door and pulled it open. "After you, ladies. There's a light right inside the door."

"Aren't you coming in?" I paused in the doorway.

"Someone needs to be the lookout. I'll fiddle around with some tools out here. That way, no one will take a second look at us."

"Good idea." I flashed him a grin and flipped the light switch.

The shed was total chaos. Boxes were piled helter skelter, some covered with canvas, others left open to the dust. Furniture was shoved into every available space. This would take days, weeks, maybe longer.

"Which ones are Maybelle's?" I called.

"They're marked with a red MS," Heath yelled back. "They're recent so should be toward the front."

"You need to organize this place." I yanked off a canvas tarp and sneezed as dust tickled my nose. We'd found the boxes we needed. I carted one over to the nearest flat service, another pile of boxes, and started digging through what remained of a woman's life. Knick knacks, clothes, everything shoved together.

"What if we're looking for the wrong thing?" Cheryl glanced up from a box of books. "Maybe that combination is to a locker at the bus station or a gym."

"If she had one of those, would there be documentation somewhere?"

She shrugged. "Maybelle didn't make a whole lot of sense."

True. I moved to another box. "We looked through her garbage, and I'm not seeing any important papers. Would those have been taken somewhere else? The manager's office, perhaps, until a next of kin was found?"

"I thought she didn't have any relatives."

"Everyone has someone, right?"

"I don't." Cheryl paused in her work. "Other than your family, I've got no one. My adoptive parents died years ago, and I have no idea who my birth parents are. When I die, that's it. My belongings will be auctioned off to pay taxes."

I gave my friend a hug. "I'll never let that happen. I'll keep everything in my garage."

"You don't have a garage." Cheryl gave a hiccupping laugh.

"Incoming." Heath poked his head through the doorway, then withdrew.

Cheryl and I stepped to the side out of direct sight of the door and peered through the crack between the door and the frame. Alice stopped next to where Heath painted planks of wood.

"With Maybelle now in the ground, we need to dispose of her things. I'd like you to cart them to the parking lot this weekend for a yard sale. The proceeds will be donated to charity. I'll make an announcement for other residents to donate items, too."

"Did Maybelle have a locked box somewhere?" Heath asked.

I smiled. He must have listened to Cheryl and my conversation. Good boy.

"We have safes for our resident's use, Heath. I'm surprised you don't know that." Alice crossed her arms and cocked her head. “Why do so many of my employees know so little about the services we offer? Does nobody read their employee packet?”

“It is rather large.” He plopped his paint brush into a quart size paint can. “I don’t have anything of value, so a safe wouldn’t be a priority for me. I’d like access to Maybelle’s if you don't mind.”

“I have no idea what the combination is. You’ll probably have to cut the lock off.”

“I’ll be by in a bit. Where are the safes?”

“The utility room between my office and the kitchen.” Her eyes narrowed. “I’ll have to be with you, you know? That’s one of the safeguards.”

“Okay, thanks.” He flashed that grin that set my stomach into flips. “I’ll be there in fifteen minutes.”

“See you then.” She studied his face for a moment, then left.

Forget the dirty boxes. Heath had scored.

“You won’t be able to take anything with her looking over your shoulder,” I said, stepping from the shed, “but make sure you take note of every single thing in there. We need to know why she wrote down the names of these four men.” I handed him the combination.

“I’ll manage.” He tapped my nose. “I’ll catch up to the two of you later.”

“Let’s soak up some sun,” Cheryl offered. “A dip in the pool will wash this dust off us.”

By the time we’d changed into our suits and taken a couple of laps in the pool, I’d expected to see Heath. I kept glancing at the pool clock. He’d been gone almost an hour. What if Alice caught him taking something and had Lawrence arrest him?

"I see your mind digging up every bad scenario possible." Cheryl pulled herself to sit on the side of the pool, her feet in the water, then grabbed my hand to hoist me up. "Stop."

"I can't help it. You know how my mind works." I kicked my feet slowly through the water. "One of those four men killed Maybelle, and most likely Dave, I know it in my gut. The trick is proving it. Maybelle knew something that got her killed."

"Yeah, but finding out what that is will drive us crazy. It's Wednesday already and I have to be back at work on Monday."

I gave her hand a squeeze. "Then, we need to solve this by the weekend."

"Sorry I'm late." Heath barged through the pool gate, letting it slam shut behind him. "Follow me to the greenhouse."

Cheryl and I glanced at each other and darted after him, wrapping pool towels around us as we went.

By the time we reached the greenhouse, I was gasping for breath. The second we entered, Heath slammed the door.

"This is the only place I could think of with a bit of privacy," he said.

"What about my cottage?"

He shook his head. "Maybelle thought her cottage might be bugged. That's next on my list to check. Also, the combination didn't work. Maybe it isn't a combination at all." He handed the slip of paper back to me and pulled some folded pages from his pocket. "You were right about her suspecting these four men of something." He spread them on my workbench.

"No matter what Marvin says, he spent seven years

in prison for almost beating a woman to death. According to Maybelle's notes, he'd threatened her a few times if she didn't stop nosing around his place. Yet, she never filed charges against him. Bob and the others also threatened her several times. Why wouldn't she report them?"

"Is being nosy enough of a motive for murder?" I glanced at the pages of handwritten notes. "She sure was careful to jot down the dates the threats were made."

"She suspected something, was looking for it, and I suspect she found it." He folded the papers. "I'm keeping these. I do not want them in your possession. It's too dangerous."

Cheryl dropped to a sitting position on the bench. "What else do we know about these men? We know that Harry lied about working for Cooper Elementary and that Marvin is a woman abuser. Just because Bob has a temper doesn't mean he's capable of murder. And what about William?"

"Bob dated Maybelle," I said. "Myrna mentioned that. For a short while, I thought maybe Maybelle had been killed out of jealousy."

"There has to be a way of finding out more about these men." Cheryl glanced between me and Heath. "Are either of you against something a bit…unethical?"

"Describe unethical." I wasn't crazy about anything illegal, immoral, or dangerous to another person. I knew my friend well, and we didn't always share the same views.

"Two of those men are attracted to me." She gave a coy smile. "It wouldn't take much to give them a little something in their drink so they answer any question I ask. I can easily find out whether they killed Maybelle."

"Absolutely not." I set my jaw. "You'll go to jail if you're caught."

"It won't be any different than a man slipping a roofie to a girl at a bar."

"I agree with Shelby." Heath shook his head. "We'll find another way."

She shrugged. "Fine. I'll go research what I can on the internet, but it won't be nearly as effective."

"While you do that, I'll find a way to get into Alice's office without her knowing. She had to have done a background check on these guys," Heath said.

That left me to distract Alice. "I'll take Alice…somewhere, and keep her occupied for as long as I can. How much time do you think you'll need?"

"Thirty minutes, max," Heath said.

Great. Now to find a way to get Alice to come with me.

I hopped off the bench. "Give me fifteen minutes to change, then head over. That will give me time to figure out a way to distract her."

Cheryl walked back to the cottage with me and booted up her laptop. "Is there a printer I can use?"

"In my room." I grabbed the capris I'd worn earlier and a floral blouse on my way to the bathroom. A quick shower, and I was ready, but still none the wiser on how I could keep Alice away from her office for thirty minutes.

I'd have to figure it out when I found her.

18

"Get rid of her," Heath hissed, his hand on the doorknob of the room next door to Alice's office.

I held out my hands. I was trying! There. I reached over and yanked the fire alarm. Shrill blasts rang through the building.

Heath gave me an exasperated look and ducked into the room next door.

"Fire." I pushed open Alice's door. "I don't smell smoke, but it's best you come check."

"Where's Heath? That's his job."

I did my best to play dumb, which lately, wasn't too hard of a task. "He took off…that way." I pointed in the opposite direction. "He said something about sending you to cottage number…thirty when I saw you." I thought that might be the farthest from where we were.

She gave a heavy sigh. "So far. Maybe I will buy him that Gator thing. I'll buy two. One for me." She shooed me from her office and pulled the door closed, locking it behind us. "Come with me."

"Shouldn't I make sure the residents get out safely?"

"Really?" She rolled her eyes. "None of them are infirm or in wheelchairs. I think they know what a fire alarm means by now. Oh, that infernal racket!"

We headed outside amidst the residents flocking to the parking lot. I prayed I wouldn't get arrested for falsely pulling the alarm, but I'd reacted in the spur of the moment. Obviously, I couldn't be trusted to make snap decisions in a moment of crisis.

I practically had to jog to keep up with Alice, which meant her fast pace might prevent me from keeping her occupied for the required thirty minutes. Think, Shelby! "Do you smell smoke?"

Alice stopped and sniffed the air. "No."

"I think it's coming from the pool area."

"Use your cell phone and call Heath. Get him here now. I'm not equipped to deal with this."

"Should I call the fire department?"

"Not until we verify we have a fire." She unlocked the gate to the pool. "Go check the changing rooms. I'll check the pump. And, hurry up." She glanced at the sky. "Not a speck of smoke. Call Heath."

I pretended to check the changing room, taking my time, horrified that we'd managed to waste less than ten minutes. While out of Alice's sight, I called Heath. "I can't keep her occupied for thirty minutes. She's starting to figure out there isn't a fire."

"That was a dumb idea."

"She told me to call you and have you meet us."

"I have what we need. I'll call Alice and tell her

it's a false alarm. Bye." Click.

I breathed a sigh of relief and rejoined Alice outside. She answered her phone, her lips stretching into a thin line. "Antiquated alarm system. Not a nice thing to deal with on the day of a resident's funeral." She marched away, leaving me to my own devices.

Consumed with guilt over pulling the alarm, I headed back to my cottage. I opened the door and froze. On my sofa, sagged Marvin and William, both clearly under the effects of a drug. I glared at Cheryl. "What did you do?"

"What I said I was going to do. I couldn't find anything incriminating on the internet. Nothing that we didn't already know, anyway."

Mercy, we were both going to jail. Me for the false alarm, her for drugging two men. "Please tell me they aren't going to die."

"Of course, they aren't. But, I'm pretty sure neither of them killed Maybelle."

"How do you know?" I peeled one of Marvin's eyes open.

"Because I asked them. Why would they lie under the influence?"

"Because they might be a murderer."

"That's why I don't feel any remorse about my method of questioning them. All we have to do now, is put them somewhere until they wake up."

"How do you propose to do that?" Both men most likely weighed over two hundred pounds each.

"I'll take a head, you take the feet. We'll put them by the pool with a beer in their hands. They were drinking when I invited them. They'll think they drank too much."

I didn't like it a bit. Still, what choice did we have? "You know, God must really be shaking His head right about now." I grabbed William's ankles.

"He's too heavy to lift and talk. Thank goodness you live close to the pool." Cheryl opened the front door, then hooked her hands under the man's arms.

With her walking backward and me forward, we managed to get him poolside with me only dropping his feet once. With him safely spread out on a lounge chair, we headed back for Marvin and ran into Heath.

He stood in the open doorway and, without turning around, said, "You didn't."

"She did." I squeezed past him. "Help us get the bigger man to the pool."

"You aren't drowning them are you?" Heath cast me a shocked look.

"Don't be silly." I grabbed Marvin's ankles. "Well, come on."

"Heath and I will carry him." Cheryl shouldered me out of the way. "You get the beer. It's in the fridge."

Why in the world did she need a case of the vile stuff? I grabbed it and hurried after them. "I'm so sorry to involve you, Heath." I thrust the beer at Cheryl. "My friend is insane and a criminal."

Cheryl grinned. "You're an accomplice."

My blood drained to my feet. "Don't remind me. Finish your diabolical plan so we can go back to the safety of my cottage."

"Please." Heath added.

"What is going on?" Alice entered the gate, her eyes widening. "Are these men drunk?" She glanced at the three of us. "Drinking is not allowed poolside. Especially with glass bottles."

"Um, these are aluminum cans." Cheryl handed them to her. "We, uh, found them like this. Yeah."

Alice stared at her as if she'd sprouted tentacles from her head. "I'll let them slide this time, seeing as how they're most likely mourning Maybelle, but if it happens again..." She made a slashing motion across her throat. "Heath, help get them home."

He groaned.

Poor man.

I felt a measure of relief in knowing that no permanent harm had been done. "I'll get my car. We'll drive them home."

Alice nodded. "I'm heading to my room. This has been the strangest day." She shook her head and left us with the chore of getting two very heavy, very drugged men into my Volkswagon.

"If you do anything like this again, I'll kill you myself." I glared at Cheryl and headed for the employee parking area behind the main building.

By the time we had the two men safely in their own homes, I was disgruntled, starving, and still had no idea what Heath had found in Alice's office. I parked my car back in its spot as the supper bell rang. I caught up with my conspirators in crime. "Grab a plate to take back to my place. If I have to wait one more—"

"Wait up, Shelby." Alice called to me the moment I stepped into the dining room.

"Fix me a plate, Cheryl." I waited for Alice.

"What are the social plans for Saturday?"

Ooops. I hadn't given them a thought.

"It's Wednesday. If people need to prepare, then they need time." She crossed her arms and raised an eyebrow.

"I'll let you know by morning."

"Now. Surely you have something rattling around in that head of yours."

"A pool party. Hawaiian theme." Great. Now, I'd have to purchase decorations and show up in a bathing suit in public.

"How fun." She clapped her hands. "I'll make the announcement while everyone is gathered for dinner." She moved away from me and to the front of the room.

As she made her announcement, Cheryl, Heath, and I, plates full, snuck out and headed for my cottage. We'd no sooner got inside and set our plates on the table, before I turned to Heath. "Well? The suspense is killing me."

"The news is there is no news." Heath leaned his chair back on two legs. "There are no files in Alice's office on those four men."

"That's impossible." What was going on here?

"Impossible or not, it's the truth."

I dropped my fork with a clatter. "We're missing something. Could Maybelle have already taken them? She did have a master key."

"Either she took them or the killer did." Heath let his chair fall forward with a thud. "Where would she have hid them?"

"Her cottage," Cheryl suggested.

"No." Heath shook his head. "That's been cleared out and cleaned. It's ready for a new tenant."

"The last place Maybelle was seen was the greenhouse." I jumped to my feet. "I bet she was there to retrieve the files." I raced outside and down the path, Heath and Cheryl thudding behind me.

"The police checked it out." Heath's key ring

provided the music for our mad dash.

"They missed something." I didn't stop until I reached our destination. "I didn't bring my keys."

Heath unclipped a ring from his belt loop and unlocked the door. "Let's split up. What was here then and is still here?"

"That bag of fertilizer, the counters," I put a finger to my lips and studied the place. "There are some other bags of seed missing, but most of it has been left. The police focused on the spot where Maybelle was found." I headed in that direction and got on my knees.

I looked first at the bottom of the counter, knowing the police would have found anything taped there. We should have asked Grandma to quiz Lawrence on anything they might have taken from the building. Next, I crawled under the bench, covering the full length, looking inside every box and crate I came across, being careful not to upset any of the tender plants I wanted to transplant. Not finding anything along the bench, I returned to Maybelle's death spot.

As unpleasant as the moment had been, I forced myself back to when I'd found her. She'd been digging!

"Cheryl, hand me a hand shovel."

"Which one?"

"I don't care. Just pick one!"

She slapped a rusty wooden handled one in my palm and squatted next to me. "What are you doing?"

"Maybelle had been digging for something when she died."

Heath joined us. "Wouldn't the police have noticed that?"

"Maybe or maybe they didn't dig deep enough." If I was going to hide something, I'd make it difficult for others to get to. When you add in Maybelle's eccentricity, well…

There! My shovel scraped against something almost a foot deep in the dirt.

"Let me." Heath took the shovel and finished uncovering a wooden box warped from water running off the above counter. "I hope the files aren't ruined."

We got to our feet, and he set the box on the counter. "Here goes nothing." He opened the box revealing a soggy mess.

While the manila file folders were intact, they were limp from water. When I opened one, the pages underneath stuck to the folder, part of one ripping. Blue and black ink ran in rivulets.

I wanted to cry. "What do we do now?"

"We take these back to your cottage, dry them out, and see if we can make anything out." Heath carefully closed the box. "It's worth a try and we're getting closer to solving this mystery."

I wished I had his optimism. In my mind, the killer stayed three steps ahead of us.

19

I woke the next morning to the sight of sheets of ink smeared paper hanging from twine extended across my living room. It might be funny if it weren't so sad and so important that we find out what Maybelle knew.

I'd just pulled my shirt over my head when someone knocked at the door. Tugging the blouse over my mid-section, checking to make sure all the buttons were lined up properly, I pulled the door open. "Alice."

"Good morning. May I speak with you?" She glanced over her shoulder. "In private?"

"Of course. Where? Cheryl is still here." Please don't say the cabin. The files are fluttering in the breeze from the door.

She thought for a moment. "It's fine if she hears."

I stepped aside and let her enter. "Coffee?"

"If you have some made, thank you." She eyed the papers hanging from the ceiling and plopped onto the sofa. "Those are the very things I want to speak with you about."

Oh, boy. I measured coffee grounds into the maker and pressed the button. "What about them?"

"Where did you find them?"

I turned. "Buried in the greenhouse under where Maybelle's body was found."

She sighed, the sound heavy in the room. "I know that, despite my uncle Ted's warning not to, that you are looking into Maybelle's murder. Oh, Shelby, I fear I'm in a terrible spot emotionally."

The weariness in her voice tugged at my heart. I sat next to her. "What's wrong?"

"I have feelings for Heath, it's not a secret, and I fear that I may have vouched for a murderer."

"Why would you say that?" I shoved down the words telling her that I, too, had feelings for our handsome handyman.

"I discovered those files missing weeks ago, before Maybelle died. Not only that, but I've been helping my uncle collect information on several of our tenants, including Heath McLeroy."

"Why Heath?"

She speared me with a glance. "Our gorgeous handyman has a past, Shelby. He spent time in jail as a teenager."

I didn't know what to say. Why hadn't he come clean with me? Weren't we close friends? "Time for what?"

"Assault." She folded her hands in her lap. "He'd gotten into a fight over a girl. That's all I know, but with a past like that…Maybelle's death…it makes him a suspect. He's the only one besides me with a master key."

"Maybelle had one. Didn't you lose a key a while back?" I pushed to my feet, the morning soured by her confession. Maybe coffee sweetened with creamer would wash the taste from my mouth. I leaned my back against the counter. "I think Maybelle took those files. She was watching Bob, Marvin, Harry, and William. In none of her things was there any mention of Heath. I think you're wrong on that regard." I squared my shoulders.

"Oh, I see." Alice paled. "You like him."

"He's a great guy." Or at least I thought so until finding out he kept such a big secret from me.

"Having a crush on a man clouds a woman's judgment."

"I don't think so in this case. Heath has been nothing but helpful in trying to find Maybelle's killer. All he wants to do is clear his name. Are you willing to help us do that or would you prefer to put the handcuffs on him right now?"

"My. My. You're like a mother lion defending her young." She hung her head. "If I help you, we can't let my uncle know."

"No problem." I poured us each a cup of coffee and without asking added vanilla flavored creamer to both, before rejoining her on the sofa. "Tell me what you know about the men in those files."

"Bob is innocent. He would never raise a hand to a woman no matter how angry he became. The man loves women." She grinned and reached for her mug. "Too much if you ask me. I think we can take him off the suspect list."

"All right." I caught Cheryl watching from the corner of my eye and motioned for her to be quiet and join us. “The others?”

“Marvin spent jail time for assault. William was fired for handing out free prescriptions, but I don’t think that necessarily makes him a killer. Harry, well, Harry is an enigma. According to him, he’s had more jobs than all of us combined.”

“He lied about being a teacher.”

She shrugged. “Harry has lied about a lot of things, but he pays his rent on time and doesn’t bother anyone.”

“What about the vampire?”

“Leroy Manning? He has a skin condition and can’t be in the sun. He’s harmless.”

I swirled a spoon in my mug. “Surely you know more than that about these men. We know as much as you do.” The glint in her eye told me she withheld information. Well, I wouldn’t help her if she didn’t plan on repaying the favor.

For several seconds we sat there and stared at each other. “Oh, very well. Alice set her mug on the coffee table hard enough to splash some of the liquid out. “Uncle Ted is trying to pin the murders on either Heath or Harry. Heath had the ease of getting close to Maybelle, and Harry is pretending to be something he isn’t.”

“Explain.” I met Cheryl’s excited gaze. It looked as if we’d been on the right track in our amateur investigations.

“You cannot tell *anyone* I told you this. Oh, Uncle Ted is going to kill me. Look to him first if I turn up dead.”

“I promise.” A glance at the clock told me we were going to be late for breakfast.

"No, I can't tell you." She jumped to her feet. "Pretend we never had this conversation." She bolted out the door as if her heels were on fire.

"That was interesting," Cheryl said. "Who do you think she was going to spill the beans on?"

"I wish I knew. Let's head to breakfast. I have a bone to pick with Heath."

"I heard, but why say anything? It happened a long time ago, Shelby. Maybe he wants a clean start."

True. "I'll think on it."

"The bigger problem seems to be the fact that you and Alice both have eyes for the same man." She grinned and bumped me with her shoulder.

I laughed. "You're right. I'm making the proverbial mountain out of a mole hill." I slipped my arm through hers as we made our way to the dining room.

It took some effort to act with Heath as if I didn't know his secret. I still felt betrayed. Friends were open with each other, weren't they? Or was it that my close friendship with Cheryl gave me an unrealistic expectation of other friendships?

I headed for the buffet, choosing pancakes with butter and powdered sugar, then chose my customary chair next to Heath. "We don't need the files anymore." I told him of most of my conversation with Alice, leaving out the fact we both liked him.

"They still suspect me?" His hand paused halfway to his mouth, a slice of bacon wiggling from his fingers.

"Unfortunately."

He groaned and tossed his bacon to his plate. "After all the hard work I've done to get my life straight." He shoved to his feet and marched out of the building.

"Nice going." Cheryl sat down.

"Yeah, this day isn't starting off well." I needed to find something to do that allowed me to do my job and snoop at the same time. Preferably something with Harry.

"What's going on in that dark head of yours?" Cheryl tossed a strawberry onto my plate.

I popped it in my mouth. "How can I get Harry to answer some questions about who he really is?"

"Let me help. As a teacher at Cooper Elementary, where he supposedly worked, I can at least get him to confess to lying about working there."

"Great idea. We'll follow him back to his cabin after breakfast. You can say you're taking a look at his bathroom for possible renovations. Anything that gets him to stop and talk to us."

I knew there was a reason I wanted her along. "There he goes." I shoved a last bite of pancake into my mouth and grabbed my plate. The last thing I needed was Alice on my case for not cleaning up after myself.

Outside, Cheryl and I made no pretense about following Harry. Not that it mattered. The man seemed to be on a mission, looking neither to the right or the left. Instead of heading to his cabin, he headed for the thick woods at the property's border.

We cast a questioning glance at each other and quickened our pace.

"Is it wise to follow?" I stopped at the trees edge. "We don't have a weapon if he turns rough."

"How bad can it be with two of us and one of him? I'm twice his size."

"In height maybe." I took my bottom lip between my teeth. If Harry did turn out to be the killer and turned on us, he couldn't take us both down. One of us would be free to run for help.

I gripped her hand and we started down the path. The early morning sunshine cut through the thick foliage overhead, dotting the path with rays of gold. A bird serenaded us. The morning was beautiful. I took a deep breath.

"What in Sam's Hill are the two of you following me for?" Harry stepped from around a thick tree.

"Oh, hello." I thought ignorance the wisest course of action. "We thought it a perfect morning for a stroll. Fancy meeting you here, though, since I do need to stop by your cottage in a bit. Shall we go now?"

Cheryl elbowed me in the rib to stop my rambling. "When it's convenient, she means."

He narrowed his eyes. "Just out for a stroll, huh?"

"Yes, sir," we said in unison.

"Seems like you're following me. What do you need at my cottage? I respect my privacy and make repairs myself."

"Alice is tossing around the idea of remodeling bathrooms and your's was chosen." I plastered a big grin on my face.

"Not interested. She can do it when I move out, which might be any day now with all the meddling you two do."

Perhaps he should buy a cabin high in the mountains instead of living in a retirement community. "I'll let Alice know. Thank you for your time." I grabbed Cheryl's arm and set off back the way we'd come. Once we were out of earshot, I said, "We have to solve this mystery before he leaves."

"If we could guarantee he'd be out of his cottage

for a bit tonight, we could do a bit of searching."

"Absolutely." But how? It was time for Heath to be the one delaying a person.

We found him scooping leaves from the koi pond and explained what we needed.

"Are you crazy?" He tossed the leaves into a bucket. "If he is the killer, I'm a sitting duck."

"No more so than Cheryl and I. You aren't going into his cottage." I crossed my arms and glared. "I occupied Alice during an illegal fire alarm. This is the least you can do."

His shoulders sagged. "I want all this to be over with."

"So, you'll do it? How?"

"I'll flood his apartment. He'll have to leave. The two of you can go in with boots on."

I hadn't expected anything so drastic. "Are you sure?"

"It's not like he'll come out if I knock on his door. I'll go loosen a pipe now while he's out for a walk. If he is the killer, and we solve this, no harm done. If we're wrong, you're helping me pay for damages."

I thrust out my hand. "Agreed. Cheryl?"

"Very well." She placed her hand on top of ours. "We'd better be right or there goes my savings."

We'd better be right or there goes my job. We pumped our hands before Cheryl went to find Grandma and I went to work replacing the flowers in front of the main building. Alice might be a bit lenient knowing I was trying to solve the murder, but she wouldn't let me skip work altogether. Not that I wanted to. Each thing I did to improve the looks of Shady Acres filled my heart with joy.

By the end of the day, a lush profusion of blooms provided a riot of color against the white siding of the building. I stretched and popped the kinks from my back. When I gathered my supplies and turned to leave, I came face-to-face with Harry.

20

"You can go look at my bathroom now." He scowled, arms folded over his paunch. "Pipe burst."

Heath had succeeded. I grinned. "I'll do that. Please leave the door unlocked."

"I don't know what you're grinning about. It isn't funny. I've been displaced." He turned and waddled off, looking more like Mr. Toad than ever.

I couldn't wait to tell Cheryl we had plans for that evening. I went back to the gardening shed and struggled with a bag of mulch until I got it into the wheelbarrow. Sometimes, even such a simple job required more muscles than I had.

"I'll get that." Officer Lawrence, in uniform, stepped forward and lifted the bag.

"Thank you." I straightened and waited for the lecture I was sure to hear.

"Alice told me that she informed you she was helping me get information on a couple of the residents."

I nodded. "I didn't force her to. I found stolen files buried in the greenhouse. She saw them drying out in my cottage and decided we should join forces."

"It's bad enough that I enlisted the help of my niece, Miss Hart, but to endanger another civilian—"

"Sir, I've been asked by friends to solve Maybelle's murder. I'm not doing anything dangerous, other than asking questions while doing my day job." I crossed my arms. "Are you going to arrest me if I continue?"

He studied me for a moment. "I'd like to, but Ida would string me up by my toenails. Let's compromise. You do nothing more than ask questions, then relay any information you find to me. Deal?"

"Deal." I kept my arms folded. I couldn't shake his hand and then snoop through Harry's cottage later. I'd have to keep my promise to only ask questions after my snoop fest.

"Somehow, I don't believe you."

"That's your prerogative." I grinned. "Tell Grandma I said hello."

"We'll see you at supper."

Uh-oh. That felt like he planned on keeping an eye on me. I'd need to find a way to sneak away without him following.

I watched him leave then hurried out to find Grandma. I'd need her help to get away from her boyfriend.

She was in my cottage giggling with Cheryl. "What's so funny?" I asked, heading for the kitchen sink to wash my hands.

"Cheryl told me of Heath's diabolical plan to get

Harry out of his home. Genius."

"Speaking of…I need your help tonight. Your dear Teddy is suspicious of me. I need you to keep him occupied the moment it gets dark so Cheryl and I can snoop in Harry's place."

She pouted. "Tough decision, sweetheart. I enjoy the man, I really do, but snooping through someone's things is a big temptation."

"Will you help me?" I wrapped my arms around her neck. "Please."

"You know I can't resist you. Yes, I'll keep him out of your way." She unfolded my arms from around her and stood. "I'd best go make myself look gorgeous. I'll try to get him to take me to supper in town. That should keep him out of your hair until nine o'clock, but no later. That's our bedtime."

"It doesn't get dark until nine." I threw myself on the sofa. "We need a new plan."

"He'll be home getting ready for bed, I promise." She kissed my cheek. "When he drops me off at home, let him see you in your pajamas. He'll think you're going to bed and not have a second thought about you snooping."

It was the only plan we had. I could snoop in baggy shorts and a big T-shirt. I'd done it plenty of times. "Thank you. You're the best."

The rest of the day passed in a blur of weeding, pruning, and mulching. By the time night hit and Officer Lawrence saw me give Grandma a goodnight kiss while in my slumber clothes, I wished I were going to bed. Exhaustion weighed me down. Instead, I clipped a small flashlight to the waistband of my shorts and told Cheryl to hurry up.

"I'm tired."

"Coming." She stepped out of her room. She was dressed in black from head to toe. "You'd better change. Those white legs of yours glow in the dark."

"Right." I quickly slipped off the shorts and slipped on a pair of dark leggings and a long-sleeved black T-shirt. I immediately started to sweat in the summer humidity. "This is awful."

"Stop complaining. At least you have boots to wear. I have to traipse through his flooded place in flip flops."

"Remember, we're trying to find something that convicts Harry and/or clears the other suspects' names. Anything of interest to give to Officer Lawrence."

"I know." Cheryl held the door open, then closed it behind us.

We stayed behind the cottages and in the shadows as much as possible until we reached Harry's cottage. Every door and window were open to help the place dry out. Still, at least an inch of water covered the floor.

"If he has anything to hide, it will be in a secret place." I stepped inside, an area rug squishing under my rain boots.

"No, duh. I thought he'd leave it out in the open. Yuck. Something floated across my toes."

"Stop whining and check the kitchen." I headed for the master bedroom.

A desk that sat against one wall seemed the logical place to look. I opened all the drawers and searched for false bottoms. Books and television taught me something at least. I didn't find any secret hiding places or files that generated my interest. In fact, I didn't find anything with Harry Weasley on them, but I did find a

Harvey Weston. Why would Harry have a letter with another man's name? Was there a suspect in the murders we didn't know about? I snapped a copy of the envelope.

After finding nothing else of interest there, I moved to the closet. The moment I opened the door I was assaulted with the strong aroma of Polo cologne. No surprise. I already knew he wore the vile scent. Still, did the man not do his laundry?

I rifled through the few items of clothing hanging on the rod, ignored the clothes in the hamper, then transferred my attention to the shelf. Plain brown boxes were lined up in a neat row. "Cheryl!"

The sound of splashing feet arrived before she did. "Find something?"

"I can't reach these boxes."

"Shorty." She gathered the five boxes in her arms and placed them on the bed.

We each opened one. Store receipts. Every box was filled with store receipts.

"Someone needs to tell this man he doesn't need receipts that are five years old." Cheryl replaced the lid on the last box. "This search was fruitless. There's nothing in the kitchen but dishes for two. Now who would want to share a meal with Harry?"

"What are you two doing in here?"

I gasped and whirled to see a tall, thin man dressed in black. His pale skin caught the moonlight through the window. The vampire! "I'm, uh, the gardener, and, uh, will be making a list of what needs fixing. Yeah." I shoved the box in my hands at Cheryl. "Nothing to help us here." I forced a smile. "Might as well put them away."

"I think you two are looting a man's home while he's staying elsewhere." Leroy Manning's dark brows lowered.

"No, no, that's not it. He, uh, asked us to get something for him." I grabbed a book from the nightstand. One glance at the title chilled my blood. *Items Around The House That Will Kill You*. I bet rat poison was mentioned. "A bit of bedtime reading."

"If you're snooping into who Harry really is, I can tell you a few things."

"Really?" I cocked my head. Could he be trusted? I knew virtually nothing about this man.

"Come out of here and take a walk with me. This is the only time of the day I can get my exercise." Leroy led us out of the cottage.

"What if he's leading us to our death?" Cheryl whispered. "He scares me."

"Hush." I clutched the book to my chest. It was the only weapon we had.

"I bet you're wondering why I only come out at night." Leroy chuckled. "I'm not a vampire. I have genetic disorder called Xeroderma pigmentosum. My skin cannot repair any damage done by ultraviolet light. Rather than suffer, I stay inside during the day."

"Oh, we weren't wondering." I bit my bottom lip.

"Everyone else does." He led us to the gazebo.

At least we were still on the property and out in plain sight of anyone happening by at nine-thirty at night. "You had information on Harry?"

"Sit, ladies." He sat on the opposite bench. "I must confess to a bit of eavesdropping and a warning. If you're going to have serious conversations, you really should close your windows." His smile was more like a shark than a friend. "I've known of your quest for days."

"Are you going to kill us?" I scooted closer to Cheryl.

"Of course not. I'm not a murderer, just a lonely man who wanders the property after most residents have gone to bed. The things I could tell you about everyone. But, we're here to talk about Harry, right?"

"We're open to hearing about William, the pharmacist, and Marvin, the wife beater," Cheryl added.

Leroy chuckled. "Marvin cries at commercials. I doubt he could kill anyone. William, well, that man is two people in one body. Get him riled up and anything could happen. As for Harry, the man isn't who he says he is."

"We know that. Alice has told us some things. We're trying to find out who he is." I wanted to throw the book, I was so frustrated. "Could we not play verbal games?"

"I don't want to make things too easy for you, Miss Hart." He crossed his arms and his ankles. "What did you take a picture of?"

"How long were you watching us?"

"From the moment you entered the cottage." He grinned again.

I swore his pointed canine teeth had grown sharper. "I took a picture of an envelope with someone else's name on it. Are you saying that name is the key?"

"That's exactly what I'm saying. Good night, ladies." He stepped from the gazebo and melted into the shadows.

"Creepy fellow." Cheryl stood. "Let's go research

the name you found. What's the book?"

I showed her the cover as we headed home. "Incriminating, don't you think?" In my mind, we were down to two suspects. I agreed with the vampire. A man who cried at sappy commercials wasn't a prime candidate to murder an old woman and a thieving fat man.

"What is that?" Cheryl pointed to something on the path, blocking us from returning to the cottage.

"A garbage bag?" I stepped closer and gasped.

Leroy Manning lay crumpled on the sidewalk, a pool of blood spreading under his head. I knelt next to him and felt for a pulse. "He's alive. Call 911."

Cheryl punched in the number on her phone. "I'm calling Officer Lawrence, too."

I pulled off my tee shirt, grateful for the tank top underneath, and pressed it to the wound on the back of Leroy's head. Someone had heard him talking to us and tried to put a stop to it. That someone could still be lurking nearby. "Cheryl, sit. You're too big of a target standing up."

She ducked. "You think his attacker is still here?"

"I'd bet my favorite pair of rubber boots they're watching us this very minute."

21

Millipedes ran up and down my spine at the thought. What if they had a gun? A knife? One of my big gardening shovels?

Leroy moaned, the sound deep in his throat. It may have been a symbol of his pain, but to me it meant life.

"Hold on, Leroy. Help is coming." I awkwardly patted his shoulder, still trying to keep my shirt firm against his wound and not think about the blood soaking the knees of my leggings.

"I don't see anyone," Cheryl whispered. "Maybe they left."

"Or maybe they want to watch Leroy die." I hissed the last word. "Keep looking."

I almost cried tears of relief when Officer Lawrence thundered down the path toward us. Behind him, came two paramedics. I was finished playing nurse. I stood, my bloody hands held out to my sides, and prepared myself for another lecture.

Officer Lawrence pulled his infernal notepad from his pocket. “You know the drill.”

I sighed and filled him in on our conversation with Leroy. “He didn’t tell us Harry’s secret, though. He likes to play games.”

“Dangerous ones.” He snapped his pad closed. “That could be you lying there, Shelby. What would I tell Ida?”

“That I got real close to catching a murderer.” I wanted to cross my arms, but my bloody hands deterred me. The spaghetti strap shirt I wore didn’t need any decoration on the white fabric. “I *am* close. I can feel it. You need to focus your investigation on Harry, whatever his real name is, and William Jamison. Stop wasting time on Heath.”

“His glove and fingerprints were all over both crime scenes. We can’t rule him out yet.”

This was the main reason I agreed to do this for Birdie. Law enforcement were blinded by rules. “Whatever. Can I go clean up now? Oh, and please let me know how Leroy is doing.”

He nodded. “Keep Cheryl by your side.”

“I will.” She was leaving Sunday. If I didn’t catch the killer by then, I’d be a sitting duck without my Amazon friend to protect me. While she looked tougher and braver than she actually was, Cheryl was better than being alone.

I turned and stared at my visibly trembling friend. “Don’t fall apart until we get home.” I grabbed her arm and dragged her behind me.

“But he could have been killed! We could have stumbled on a dead body.”

“It wouldn’t have been my first one, unfortunately.

Buck up." I unlocked the door to my cottage and let her go in ahead of me.

"Eeew. You're covered in blood." She gagged and dashed for the bathroom.

I discarded on the way to my room, thankful to have the sticky clothes off me. The leggings went in the garbage. I adjusted the water in the shower and stepped in, raising my face to the spray. Not only because it was soothing, but so I wouldn't see Leroy's blood wash down my drain.

By the time the water cooled, I had regained most of my composure and hoped Cheryl had, too. I stepped out of my room and spotted Heath. He got to his feet and held out his arms.

I ran to him, wrapping my arms around his waist and laid my head on his shoulder. We didn't need to speak. It meant enough that he came to check on me.

After a few minutes, he held me at arm's length. "Are you all right? Cheryl is a mess."

"I'm fine." I forced a smile. Had he comforted her, too? Thinking that he had ruined the moment for me. I slipped from his grasp and fell to the sofa. "He was going to tell us a secret about Harry and a man named Harvey Weston. But, he laughed and said we had to figure it out. The next thing we knew, he was bleeding on the sidewalk."

"It was awful." Cheryl sat in a stuffed chair, holding a pillow to her chest. "Shelby was amazing, though. She used her shirt as a bandage and knelt right there in Leroy's blood," she made a choking sound, "and didn't think anything about it. I was useless."

"Not completely. You were there for a show of force and moral support."

She rolled her eyes. "What's our next step?"

"It looks like we need to find out what Harry and William are hiding," Heath said.

"We've been saying that. I feel like a broken record." I propped my feet on the coffee table. I took a deep breath. "We need to bait them."

"No." Heath shook his head. "If anyone does, it will be me."

"It needs to be two people, together." I speared him with a glance. "Maybelle and Dave were alone when they were killed. If we bait these men, make them believe we have something on them and that someone else also knows the same information, it will be safer."

"You've gotten quite good at this," Cheryl said, looking impressed. "What happened to my mousy little friend?"

"She stared death in the face."

"All right." Heath took my left hand in his. "We'll do this. We'll start spreading the word that you two, and me, know who killed Maybelle and Dave. Hint that we've gone to the authorities but that the physical evidence is hidden in a safe place. That should draw out the killer."

"Then what?" Cheryl leaned forward. "Can we carry a gun in this place?"

I shook my head. "No, I do remember reading that in those papers on the table. If anyone has a gun, then it's a safe bet they're the killer."

"Can we buy a Tazor then? I need some kind of weapon. I may be tall, but I can still be beaten, abducted, or killed."

"Install the police siren app on your phone. You press that and everyone within a hundred feet will know something's up." I stood. "I'm exhausted. We'll talk more tomorrow. Saturday night is the pool party. It would be wonderful if this was wrapped up by then."

"You've been here less than a month. If you solve this by Saturday, you're pure genius." Heath placed a tender kiss on my forehead, tossed Cheryl a wave, and let himself out.

I grinned. Maybe he did care for me. Still, like he said, I hadn't been here long. Anything could happen. Look at my almost wedding.

"Want to share a bed like old times?" The thought of sleeping alone after finding Leroy did not appeal to me in the least.

"Gladly." Cheryl followed me to the master bedroom. Once we lay down, pulling the sheet up to our chins like we did after watching a scary movie as kids, she asked, "Who do you think killed Dave and Maybelle?"

"The logical choice is William, if Leroy is correct about the man's vicious nature. It's hard to imagine Mr. Toad as a brutal killer, but stranger things have happened in the world."

"What if it isn't either one of them? It's possible we're chasing a rabbit down a very deep hole."

That's what I was afraid of.

~

At breakfast the next morning, I studied the residents a bit harder than usual. One of them tried to kill Leroy last night. Funny thing. Neither of the main suspects were at breakfast.

The main topic of conversation was about me finding Leroy knocked out. Speculation ran from him falling down drunk and a serial killer running amok.

Alice was also strangely absent. I didn't know what to make of that. She hadn't skipped a single meal since I started working there.

"What's wrong?" Heath sat next to me. "You looked like you have something very unpleasant on your mind."

"I'm wondering where Alice is. Since she's helping her uncle, she might be the next target. She lives in an apartment upstairs, right?"

"Yeah."

"Will your master key work on her room?"

"Of course." He shoved a slice of bacon into his mouth. "Let's go check on her."

I grabbed a banana nut muffin, waved at Cheryl who had just entered, then left with Heath. I'd expected Cheryl to follow us, but she'd shaken her head and rubbed her stomach. Few things interrupted her from eating.

Heath opened a door that had a sign that said private. In front of us was a flight of stairs. "No elevator here."

"I can handle one flight."

Our steps echoed on the concrete stairs. A sense of foreboding came over me. I couldn't help but feel as if the stairs led to something I'd rather not see. Normally, I chalked such feelings up to an active imagination, but the last two weeks had changed all that.

We stepped out of the stairwell onto indoor/outdoor carpet designed to hide any stain amidst its myriad of swirls and colors. One door was across from us with a brass placard that said, "Manager."

I stepped back and let Heath knock. When he received no answer, he tried one more time, then inserted his key into the lock. "If she gets mad, we'll explain that we were worried." He waited for me to give him the go ahead with a nod, then pushed the door open.

Furniture lay on its side. Papers fluttered from a breeze through an open window. I glanced outside. A ladder leaned against the building. "Alice?"

"Stay with me." Heath pushed me behind him and moved to the bedroom.

Blankets were puddled on the floor. The top mattress leaned against the bed. The closet door hung open revealing clothes pulled off hangars.

"Someone was looking for something," I said.

"I wonder if they found what they were looking for." Heath yanked open the bathroom door.

A wide-eyed Alice, her mouth taped and her hands and feet bound with duct tape, stared at us from the bathtub. She started shrieking behind the tape as I pushed Heath aside to get in.

I pulled open drawers in search of something sharp and found a pair of cuticle scissors. "Hold still so I don't cut you."

Her eyes cast daggers as she glared up at me. The moment the tape was cut away, she started spitting like a cat. "This is all your fault." She held up her hands for me to cut away the tape.

"How is your getting tied up my fault?" I was tempted to leave her trussed up like a turkey.

"Because the person who did this said it was." With her hands free, she started tugging at the binding around her feet. "They were going to kill me."

"You saw who did this?"

"No." She looked at me as if I were the densest

person on the planet. “They hit me from behind. I didn’t come to until I was in the tub. As they were leaving, they yelled, ‘if that nosy gardener hadn’t of been telling people I knew things I shouldn’t, I wouldn’t have been involved.’ What did you tell who?”

“I didn’t…oh. I only mentioned your name in passing to Leroy. Who, by the way, is in the hospital. You should count your blessings rather than blame me.”

“I told you the things I told you in confidence.” She glanced over my shoulder. “Oh, hello, Heath. Thank you for coming to rescue me.” She held her hand out to him.

He gave me a wry smile and helped her from the tub. “Coming to look for you was Shelby’s idea. I didn’t realize you were missing.”

“True story.” I folded my arms. “When I didn’t see you at breakfast, I realized something was up. Brace yourself before leaving this room. It isn’t a pretty sight. Why didn’t they kill you?” The person didn’t seem adverse to extinguishing a life.

“Because one of the cleaning girls knocked on the door and scared them away.” She shoved me out of the way and darted from the room. She screamed and threw the one remaining unbroken item across the room. A lamp.

“What were they looking for?” Heath shoved the mattress into place.

“Those stupid soggy files, more than likely.” She kicked a pillow, then grabbed her toe.

I moved the offending item, then smiled at the sight of a large lead vase hidden there. It served her right for having a temper tantrum. “Those files are unreadable."

"This could be exactly the bait we were looking for," Heath said.

"What are you talking about?" Alice perched on the bed. "Where is my cell phone? She dug under the blankets. "Ah ha. I'm calling Uncle Ted."

"We've decided to let the killer think we have something on him, or her."

"That will draw the murderer out of hiding."

I grinned. "That's the plan."

22

I chose not to wait for an update on Leroy and knocked on his door the next day about mid-morning. Alice had told me that the hospital had released him after a night of observation.

A very groggy Leroy opened the door and squinted against the sunlight. “Come in before you kill me.”

I stepped into an immaculate, sparsely furnished cottage. If not for a plate of half-eaten eggs and bacon on the dinette table, I’d wonder whether anyone lived there. “How are you feeling?”

He shrugged. “Like I was hit over the head.”

Pretending like I knew what that felt like, I nodded. “Did you happen to get a look at your attacker?”

“Not a peek. They came up behind me like a coward.” He picked up his plate and carried it to the sink. “This is why I avoid people.”

I glanced at his sofa, hoping he’d offer me a seat. He didn’t. “Do you meet many people on your nightly walks?”

“A few, why?” He faced me.

"We, Cheryl, Heath, and I, think you were targeted because someone was listening to our conversation. Alice was also attacked last night. We want to use this to our advantage. We want you to help us spread the word that I have some files in my possession, and have left copies with someone else, that gives the identity of the murderer."

"You're asking to be killed." He crossed his long arms.

"I'm asking for this to all be over while I have backup. Cheryl leaves on Sunday." I eyed the sofa again. "Helping us will take the bulls-eye off your back."

"Hopefully, but not guaranteed. Very well, I'll do it. There is little enough for me to do for entertainment." He held the door open for me. "If you don't mind, I'd like to rest now."

"Thank you, Leroy." I stepped outside and sighed. I didn't know whether he would help or not, but I'd done my assignment for that morning. Now, with the lunch bell ringing, it was time for part two.

I met Cheryl and Heath at the door. Forming a united front, we stepped into the dining room, glanced around long enough for the residents to notice us, then headed for our usual table. Now that we had everyone's attention, I whispered as loud as possible, "It's taken care of. The files have been delivered."

Cheryl giggled behind her hand. "This is all so James Bondish."

I glared and shook my head, kicking her under the table. "If something happens to me, make sure You-Know-Who passes on the information."

"This is ridiculous," Heath said in a much lower

whisper. "No one with half a mind will think you serious."

"Then why do we have everyone's attention?" I raised my eyebrows.

"Because you're making a spectacle of yourself. A cute one, but…" He stood. "I'm getting my food."

"He seems a bit out of sorts this morning." Cheryl also left to get her lunch.

"What in the world are the three of you talking about?" Grandma sat next to me. "Everyone is buzzing about what happened to Leroy and Alice, now this."

I quietly filled her in on our plan. "Make sure you tell Ted that this is just a ploy."

"He won't like it one bit." Grandma tapped a manicured nail on the tabletop.

"I'm hoping he'll stick close, but out of sight. I don't want to get hit on the head or shoved into a closet."

"I'll do my best to get him to see the logic behind this crazy scheme of yours. Are you going snooping any time soon?"

"No, I have a tropical theme party to get ready for." My stomach rumbled. I headed for the buffet.

"You found out something?" Birdie leaned close.

"Perhaps." I gave her my most secretive smile.

"Well? Spill it. Who killed Maybelle?" Her voice rose.

"Shh." I put a finger to my lips. "That's not something I can discuss here."

"You're digging a six foot hole," Heath hissed on his way past.

"What does he mean by that?" Birdie stretched to her full height which was a good two inches shorter than me. "Am I in danger?"

"If you persist on questioning me, you might be." I used a pair of tongs to grab two slices of bacon for my BLT.

She skedaddled.

I finished making my sandwich, grabbed a fruit cup, and then rejoined the others at the table. "Mission accomplished."

Heath, a muscle ticking in his jaw, shook his head. "I don't think I can do this. It's too dangerous. Look at you!" His gaze scanned me from head to toe. "Anyone could drape you over their shoulder and take off."

"My petite stature has nothing to do with this."

"It has a lot to do with it. I'm scared, Shelby." He heaved a sigh and stared at his plate. "Cheryl, Ida, would you excuse us, please?"

They grabbed their plates and switched tables.

Heath turned and took both of my hands in his. His eyes pierced mine. "I haven't known you long, Shelby Hart, but you mean a lot to me. The idea of you putting yourself in danger this way makes me crazy. I'm not afraid for myself, but I'm terrified of something happening to you."

"You asked me to help clear your name."

"Not by using yourself as bait." He lowered his voice as it had started to rise.

I could only hope that the people watching us thought we were discussing the information we might possess and not having a lover's spat. I wasn't ready for that.

"Two weeks before I started working here, I stood in a church, ready to get married. The groom texted me and called it off. I broke my contract with the elementary school where I worked and applied here. I'm not ready for a relationship, Heath. I only want your friendship." Tears stung my eyes.

"I'm not asking you to marry me." He released my hands and ran his fingers through his hair. "I can't help how I feel any more than you can. Relationship or not, I'm still afraid of this crazy plan."

I opened my mouth to say something, but had nothing to say other than I was sorry. That didn't seem appropriate, so I focused on my lunch. "I'll be careful," I managed to get out.

"Yeah. Like Maybelle and Dave." He got up and marched away.

Appetite gone, I shoved my plate away and put my face in my hands. Normally, I'd hide my emotions until I was alone, but I wanted people to see me, to wonder, to make assumptions. It was hard being in the public eye when my insides were being ripped apart.

When I thought enough time had passed where I wouldn't run into Heath when I went back to work, I stood and carried both our plates to the side board. Ignoring the curious glances my way, I pushed open the double glass doors and made my way to the pool house where I had stashed the decorations for tomorrow night's party. Cheryl and Grandma had promised to help, but I didn't want to wait for them. I had too much on my mind to process through and needed some time alone.

I dragged out a box of blow up palm trees to the pool deck, then went back for leis I'd ordered, paper pineapple lanterns and tiki lamps. I'd make Shady Acres look as much like the tropics as I could.

With my arm full, I turned. Heath took the box

from me and set it on the ground before cupping my face with his hands. "I'm sorry." He leaned his forehead against mine. "I don't have the right to make demands on you or tell you what to do."

I wrapped my arms around his waist. "It feels nice to have someone care. I behaved badly."

"Will you let me help you decorate?"

"Will Alice let you?"

"Forget about her." He ran his hands down my arms and gave me a crooked smile. "You and I are only friends, right?"

"Right." I returned his smile. I was truly blessed to have such a friend.

"Oh, goody, you made up." Grandma clapped her hands. "So sweet. Now, what do you want me to do?"

I laughed and pulled out of Heath's embrace. "There are tablecloths in here. Heath will set up the folding tables. If you can use the clips in there to make sure the cloths stay in place, that would be awesome. Cheryl, I'll need your help stringing the paper pineapples."

"Gotcha!" She grabbed the needed box and set to work.

Soon, the four of us worked like ants to transform the pool area into a tropical paradise. Several residents tried to peek in on our progress, but we ran them off. It would be better if the decorations were a surprise.

"This is looking very nice." Alice locked the gate behind her. "You were a true find as an employee, Shelby. Not only are the grounds shaping up, but the residents have only good things to say about your social get togethers."

"That's great news. I try." I turned away as she

approached Heath. Regardless of his growing feelings for me, Alice wanted a relationship. It was better that he focus on her.

"I bought a new swimsuit for tomorrow," she cooed. "The top is made with artificial coconuts."

Cheryl made gagging motions behind her.

I stifled a laugh. I'd chosen a tropical dress rather than a suit. Not planning on going in the water, I'd be less self-conscious.

"That's nice." Heath lifted a box of paper dishes and set it on one of the tables. "Are you here to help? Because these could be organized."

"Oh, no. I have plenty of work to do. Y'all have fun." She caressed his cheek and left.

"Brazen hussy," Grandma said under her breath.

This time I did laugh. There was nothing like dear Grandma speaking her mind to cheer me up.

"You ought to make her stop drooling over your man."

"He isn't my man, Grandma. I'm not ready."

"Oh, pooh. Donald was nothing more than a trial run that went bad. He was a rusty old Chevy. Heath is a Mercedes."

"Don't push."

"I just want you to be happy."

"I am happy. I have a great job, you live close by, I see Mom on a regular basis, and I'm making the world these people live in a prettier place. What more could I ask for?" I set a champagne fountain in the center of the table designated for drinks.

"You need a man who cherishes you."

I glanced to where Heath helped Cheryl secure the string of lanterns. "I may have that already in the very capacity I can handle."

Although I knew he couldn't hear me, it was as if he felt my gaze. Heath turned and gave me a wink. Everything wrong with the world melted away until Grandma spoke again.

"Don't go anywhere without Cheryl or Heath. Not after your little charade in the dining room. It was bad enough when I was shoved into the tool shed. We all know you won't be able to keep your mouth shut long enough not to be killed for your smart mouth." She patted my shoulder and left the pool area, obviously finished helping.

I frowned. Of course I knew when to stop talking. If a person told me to shut up or they'd kill me, you could be darn toot'n I was going to be quiet.

"Psst."

I searched the bushes behind me.

Birdie peered through the Rhododendrons. She waved me over. "I've done what you wanted. I told everyone within hearing distance that you knew who the killer was and would be talking to the police as soon as possible."

My blood ran cold. "That isn't exactly what I said to you. Birdie, I don't know anything." Lord have mercy, I'd be dead before our pool party tomorrow.

"That's exactly what you said."

"It's all a ruse to draw the killer out." I wanted to strangle her myself. "Not only have you put me in dire danger, but yourself."

"Not me. I'm leaving for a few days and staying in a hotel." She let the branches fall back into place, calling out, "Good luck!"

23

*T*he plan we'd concocted to catch a killer seemed a bust. It had been almost twenty-four hours and no one had been confronted, abducted, or almost killed. Despite the crazy idea having originated in my mind, I was relieved.

I smoothed the skirt of my tropical sundress, slid my feet into sandals sporting a huge flower on top of them, and stuck a silk hibiscus in my hair. I was ready for some tropical fun. I grabbed a wicker handbag big enough to stuff a medium sized dog into and joined Cheryl in the living room.

My eyes widened and I laughed harder than I had in days. She wore a green grass skirt that fell to her knees and the largest coconuts on her chest that man could make.

"Do you like?" She twirled, revealing bright yellow shorts underneath the skirt. "If Alice can dress like this, why can't I? I have a lot more curves." She flashed a grin. “I just wish there were some men my age attending this shindig.”

“Find yourself a rich sugar daddy and live the rest of your life with no worries.”

“Let’s survive until tomorrow first. What’s the giant bag for?”

“Door prizes. I have one of those hula girls that dance on a car’s dashboard, a bobble head doll, a coconut bird feeder, and some mango flavored Moscato as the big prize.” I spotted the slip of paper with the numbers I’d once thought was a lock combination. I slipped it into my bag. Maybe Alice knew what they were.

Wait a minute. I pulled the paper back out again. “Cheryl, do you remember that code we used to use to write notes to each other in class?”

“Yeah? The one with the letters of the alphabet actually being the letter of the one after it?”

“I think that’s what this is.” I showed her the numbers.

She grabbed a pencil from the table and the back of an envelope. Seconds later, she’d decoded the message. “Weasley is Weston. Then the letters wp. What do those stand for?”

“Witness Protection! I saw it in a movie once. What would Weasley need protection from?”

“I don’t know, but I’m going to take my laptop to the party.” She grabbed it from her room. “Let’s go find this murderer.” She fixed me with a stern look. “I might look tough, but I’m really that little girl who’s afraid of thunder. We don’t get separated, understand?”

“I agree.” I forced a smile. Tonight was the night. If Harry didn’t come to us, we’d go to him.

Side-by-side, like mismatched bookends, we marched to the pool. The party wasn't scheduled to start for another hour, but we arrived early so I could make sure everything was as it should be. The wind had participated the night before, for the most part, and I decided to leave the few silk flowers that had blown into the pool there to drift among the floating lights.

Melodramatic or not, this might be my last night on earth. I wanted it to be special. I slid my giant purse under a table, found a spot for Cheryl to sit and search the internet, then greeted Heath, resplendent in a grass skirt of his own, with a smile. He'd chosen to go shirtless and took my breath away with his six pack abs and muscular arms.

I grabbed a silk lei and draped it over his neck. "Aloha." I planted a quick kiss on his lips. "You look gorgeous."

He laughed. "I don't hold a candle to you, my tropical princess."

I took his hand and pulled him to the side. "We figured out what the numbers mean. The ones we thought were a combination. Harry Weasley is really Harvey Weston, and he's in the witness protection program. Cheryl is researching him now."

"That's awesome. How did you figure it out?"

I explained the code Cheryl and I had used as children. "It's very simple and effective. Most people might not think of it."

"You're a smart girl. What do you need me to do to help prepare for the guests?"

"More chairs, I think. There are some in the pool area. Maybe another table or two. I think all the residents are coming."

As the sun began to set, residents started trickling into the pool area, filling the air with chatter, oohs, and ahs. My decorations were a hit. With my cheeks sore from grinning, I welcomed each and every person who came through the gate. Everyone except Harry, err Harvey. He was a no show.

Cheryl grabbed my arm and pulled me behind a blow up palm tree. "He's an accountant for one of the biggest mobs in the country. Or he was, anyway. He turned on them, putting several big wigs behind bars. I bet Maybelle found out and he killed her. Then, Dave found Maybelle's information when he was stealing from her, and he was killed."

"Very astute." Something hard rammed me in the ribcage. "Now, without turning around, walk out the gate and meet me on the flagstone walk. If you don't, that sweet little grandmother of yours gets shot. I have her in my sights as we speak."

I glanced to where Grandma entered on Officer Lawrence's arm. I did my best to pretend nothing was amiss and slipped my hand in Cheryl's. Together, we waltzed out the gate as if we were on a Sunday stroll.

Harvey showed his gun the moment we stepped into sight. Without saying another word, he motioned for us to walk ahead of him.

"Where are we going?" I started to glance over my shoulder and received another jab with his gun for my trouble.

"The lake. So sad, really. They'll find the two of you floating with the fishies."

"What excuse are you going to give? Why leave the pool party, which I'm in charge of, to swim in the dirty lake?" He really needed a better plan.

"I'll think of something. Maybe I'll tie you up in the boat house and set it on fire. Yeah, I like that idea better. No more talking or I'll shoot you right here."

Drowning might be less painful. There had to be a way out of our situation. I wish Heath hadn't been in the pool house when we left. He would have known right away something was wrong.

"Stay." Harvey barked the command as if he were speaking to a couple of dogs. He unlocked a shiny new padlock from the boat house door and ushered us inside. "Sit on the floor. Hey, coconut girl, you first."

Cheryl glared at him and plopped down, her grass shirt flaring around her. "You're an evil man."

"I've been called worse. Miss Hart?"

I exhaled sharply and sat with my back against Cheryl. "So, were we correct in our assumptions as to why you killed Maybelle? I mean, if you're going to kill us, you might as well answer our questions."

"Do you realize how cliché that is, Miss Hart?" He dug around on a rough wood counter, finally locating a long length of boating rope. He wrapped the rope around and around us until breathing became difficult. "I suppose it doesn't hurt. You've already figured out who I really am. My original target wasn't Maybelle. No one would have believed that crazy old woman anyway. No, I was after Alice." He said it as if killing the wrong woman was the saddest thing ever.

"The rat poison was left in Alice's water bottle. Maybelle, the sticky fingered woman, stole the bottle and drank."

"But the box was next to Maybelle. Her gums were swollen. Was she wearing her own teeth?"

"The box of poison was already in the greenhouse.

I didn't put it there, but I didn't move it either. It worked out quite well except for the fact that Alice, the cop's niece, is still walking free and trying to discover who I really am." He scowled. "How do I know whose teeth was in that crazy broad's mouth?"

"But…Maybelle's shoulders had bruises. Like someone held her down."

"I don't know anything about that. She probably hurt herself crawling into a tight space."

I needed to try another tactic to keep him talking. "Alice knows everything."

"I doubt it." He leaned close to my face. "Who is your constant companion? Who would you have told your secrets to? Miss Coconut here. Take the both of you out, and voila! I've closed the mouths of those knowing the truth."

How did he miss my friendship with Heath? Or the time I spent with Grandma? I was grateful he had, but the man really wasn't as smart as he thought he was.

"You two sit tight. I'll be back later to set the night on fire. Can't do it while everyone is awake, now can I? They'll come rushing to your rescue and ruin everything. I'll tell the guests that the big gal got food poisoning and the sweet Miss Hart took her to Urgent Care." He slipped out the door and locked us in, covering us with darkness.

"Do you think anyone will hear us if we scream?" Cheryl asked.

"No. We're too far away." Tears clogged my throat. "Just when I was thinking how stupid he was to think you were the only person I told, he came up with the brilliant idea of food poisoning. Anyone who knows you will believe that you ate something you shouldn't."

"What's that supposed to mean?"

"You like to eat."

"We're about to die a horrible death and you're making fun of me."

"No, I'm not." I struggled against the rope. "I'm only saying how the story makes sense."

"Fine." She sagged. "It's true. I love food."

"Can you see anything?"

"Just a sliver of light through a crack in the door."

"That's good. We know where the door is. Before he locked us in, did you see anything that might cut this nylon rope?"

"No. Before we die, I want you to know how much I love you and what a true friend you've been all these years."

"I love you, too. We aren't going to die." Not if I had something to say about it. "Think, Cheryl. We have two hours to figure out how to get free. The party will be over then, and we'll burn."

"Right. Let's scoot my direction."

She ended up pulling me more than I participated in the scooting. When we came up against several crates we had no hope of opening, we moved in the opposite direction. I'd bet my favorite rain boots there was something sharp on top of the counter. Reaching it was the problem.

"Brace our backs against each other. Maybe we can push to our feet," I said.

"Good idea." Cheryl shoved so hard, I stumbled forward, almost taking us both down.

"Careful. Remember, how much bigger you are."

"Right. I need to remember how delicate you are."

I then remembered that, although we were best

friends and loved each other immensely, we often snapped during times of stress and could come at each other like rabid dogs. I decided to remain kind and take a gentle approach. "It's all right. We'll do better next time."

"Don't talk to me as if I'm a third grader, Shelby!"

"I'm not. I'm trying to stay nice!"

"Don't yell at me!"

"I'm not!" By this time we were on our feet tugging and pulling against each other. "Hey, we did it."

"We're quite the team."

We hobbled to the workbench. "I can't see anything. Since you're taller, see if you can feel around the counter top," I told her.

"It's going to hurt when the rope pulls against you."

"That's okay. I can deal with pain if it gets us out of here." I sniffed. "Do you smell that?"

"He's early!" Cheryl yanked against me.

My feet slid from underneath me, and we crashed to the floor. Smoke seeped through every crack and crevice in the boat house walls. There was no honor from murderers.

24

The rope slipped around me. It was loosening! "Quick, Cheryl, wiggle some more." We were getting out of there. That's what Harvey got for tying someone of my size to someone of Cheryl's.

"Give…me…a second. Your elbow…knocked the air…from me."

"If we don't hurry, there won't be any air to worry about."

By the time we freed ourselves, smoke filled the boathouse. I crawled to the counter where Harvey had found the rope and pulled to my feet. Trying not to breathe too deeply, I felt around the rough surface for something to break the lock on the door. Tears streamed down my face.

A loud banging came from behind me. I turned.

Cheryl kicked the wall with all the strength she possessed, stopping every few seconds to gasp for breath. Her efforts made little progress.

My hand wrapped around the handle of a sledgehammer. I thrust it into my friend's hands.

She drew back and whacked the wall. Again and again until the crack between the boards widened. If we could stay conscious long enough, we might make it out alive.

With her pounding on the wall, I chose that moment to deliver an eleventh hour prayer. Something I should have thought of days ago. My tendency to race toward danger surprised me. As a child, I'd been shy, a loner, content with one or two friends. Now, I was surrounded by multitudes of people who liked me, a few who loved me, and one who wanted me dead. I was treading on foreign soil.

"Shelby!" An even louder banging than what Cheryl made came from the door of the boat house. Heath had come to the rescue. Hopefully, with help.

"In here!"

The door flung open. Heath stood outlined by moonlight. Behind him stood Harvey, a board in his hand.

"Behind you!"

Heath turned.

Harvey swung, connecting with Heath's head.

I lunged forward, tackling the round, evil man to the ground. "Cheryl, help me!" I wouldn't be able to hold him myself, but with my friend's help, the man was going nowhere.

Cheryl pinned his arms to his side and sat on him. "Go check on your man."

I scurried to Heath's side as Officer Lawrence and Grandma raced toward us. Officer Lawrence barked orders on his hand held radio while Grandma knelt beside me.

Heath moaned, relieving most of my fears. "You're okay."

I gave something between a sob and a laugh. "You're the one we need to be worried about." A fit of coughing over took me, increasing the tears running down my cheeks.

Paramedics converged on the scene. One of them slapped an oxygen mask over my face, then gently moved me to the side so he could tend to Heath.

Officer Lawrence wrestled with Cheryl, trying to get her off of Harvey and to stop punching him. She screamed with each punch and said several choice words that darkened the officer's face.

A second paramedic gave her a shot of something in the arm, then administered oxygen to the drugged, but still angry Cheryl. Once she was off the half-conscious killer, Officer Lawrence cuffed him.

"Good job," he said, hauling Harvey away.

"Heath was a maniac once we realized Harvey's story about food poisoning wasn't true." Grandma wrapped her bony arms around me.

"How did you know?"

"We called the hospital and every Urgent Care after finding Cheryl's laptop still up and running. It wasn't hard to figure out from that point. Teddy sent out a search party and here we are."

"Yes, here you are." I'd never been so glad to see someone in my whole life.

The paramedics hoisted Heath on to a gurney. "Just for the night," one of them said.

"I'm going with him." I pulled free of Grandma's embrace.

"Of course you are. I'll watch out for Cheryl, although I have no idea how to get a drugged Amazon back to the cottage." She eyed my large friend with despair.

I laughed. "You'll figure it out." I landed a kiss on her cheek as firemen dragged hoses toward the boat house. It was a total loss, I was sure, since flames no longer nibbled around the bottom, but now devoured the dry wood to the rooftop.

Oxygen masks removed, Cheryl no longer spewing obscenities, the medical responders prepared to leave. I shuffled after them, still gasping out the occasional cough.

One of paramedics stopped me as I followed them to the ambulance in the parking lot and went to climb inside. "You refused further medical attention."

"I'm going with him."

"Only immediate family, ma'am. I'm sorry."

"But I feel faint. I changed my mind. I need medical attention. The oxygen didn't work. I'm going to fall." I put a hand to my forehead and closed my eyes, opening one just enough to see the man's scowl.

"Please let her come." Heath stretched a hand out toward me.

I grinned and bounded inside, sitting on a bench next to his gurney. "Are you better?" A white bandage wrapped around his head matched the pallor of his skin.

"Hold my hand and I will be."

I slid my hand in his and kissed the back of it. "Thank you for saving me."

"You scared me, Shelby. I have a feeling you're going to keep me on my toes for a long time."

I hoped so. Shady Acres had become my home. I

didn't want to live anywhere else or with a different group of people. "I think I'll leave the sleuthing to the professionals."

"At least until the next mystery."

I gulped. "You think there will be another one?" I didn't think I could go through it again. Still, a small thrill shot through me. The adrenaline rush of trying to outwit a killer could easily become an addiction.

"There is always something going on at Shady Acres."

The ambulance pulled up at the Emergency Room doors. Waiting for us was Officer Lawrence and my mother. One looked relieved, the other serious.

I chose my relieved, eyes filled with tears mother. She opened her arms and I rushed into them like a small child looking for comfort. Her soothing murmurs and soft pats on the back eased the stress and fear of the last few hours.

Officer Lawrence cleared his throat. "I have a few questions, Miss Hart."

"Of course, you do." I grabbed Heath's hand as he was being wheeled past. "You'll have to follow us. Mom?"

"I'll be right here waiting for you."

We were taken to a curtained alcove number four. Heath was rolled into place. I sat in the vacant chair next to him.

"Miss Hart, the doctor will check you out after Mr. McLeroy," the paramedic said. "If you still need the attention."

I smiled. "Thank you for letting me come with you."

He muttered something to the effect that he didn't

have a choice and left us.

I transferred my attention to Officer Lawrence. "Your turn."

"You're awfully cocky for someone who almost burned to death."

"Almost being the key word here." I shuddered. "We were free of our bindings and working on getting out when Heath found us."

"I saw the smoke," Heath said. "Hard not to when the moon lights up smoke like a silver cloud."

Officer Lawrence pulled out his infernal notepad. "You know the drill. Start from the beginning."

I told him how Birdie had come to me for help, how we'd snooped through Maybelle's things, thinking the numbers were a combination and realizing they were actually a childish code. Then, Cheryl finding out Harvey was in witness protection. "What I'd like to know is why he killed to keep that information secret. Shouldn't he have just gone to y'all?"

Officer Lawrence heaved a sigh. "He was still working for the mob, we discovered."

"Did you know that your niece was his actual target, not Maybelle?"

His eyes widened. "He told you that?"

"Yes, sir. He didn't like her snooping into his private affairs. The man obviously has no regard for human life."

"Obviously." His lips twitched.

"Did you ever find my ladybug gloves?"

"Yep. In Harvey's cottage. We were coming to arrest him when we found out you were missing." He snapped his notepad closed. "You were a big help with this case, Shelby, but for the sake of us all, especially your grandmother, stay out of police investigations."

Since I couldn't make that promise, I just smiled.

The End

Check out book 2, Path to Nowhere, by scanning this code.

ABOUT THE AUTHOR

www.cynthiahickey.com

Cynthia Hickey is a multi-published and best-selling author of cozy mysteries and romantic suspense. She has taught writing at many conferences and small writing retreats. She and her husband run the publishing press, Winged Publications. They live in Arizona and Arkansas, becoming snowbirds with three dogs. They have ten grandchildren who keep them busy and tell everyone they know that "Nana is a writer."

Made in the USA
Las Vegas, NV
17 October 2024

97059130R00121